I0749171

The Dead Go Fast

Also by James C. Wilson from Sunstone Press:

Santa Fe, City of Refuge: An Improbable Memoir of the Counterculture
Hiking New Mexico's Chaco Canyon: The Trails, The Ruins, The History

The Fernando Lopez Santa Fe Mystery Series:

Ghost Canyon
The Dead Go Fast
Painted Skull Ranch
Peyote Wolf
Smokescreen

The Dead Go Fast

A Fernando Lopez Santa Fe Mystery

James C. Wilson

Santa Fe

Sunstone books may be purchased for educational, business, or sales promotional use. For information please write: Special Markets Department, Sunstone Press, P.O. Box 2321, Santa Fe, New Mexico 87504-2321.

eBook 978-1-61139-673-7

Library of Congress Cataloging-in-Publication Data

Names: Wilson, James C., 1948- author. | Wilson, James C., 1948- Fernando Lopez Santa Fe mystery.
Title: The dead go fast / James C. Wilson.
Description: Santa Fe : Sunstone Press, [2022] | Series: A Fernando Lopez Santa Fe mystery | Summary: "When the estranged wife of the Santa Fe mayor is found murdered at Jimmy Mackey's studio on Canyon Road, detective Fernando Lopez launches a politically fraught investigation of Mackey, the mayor, and others connected to the murdered woman, but then after Mackey is murdered, Lopez himself becomes a target, forcing Lopez to reassess his investigation and rethink his idea of justice"-- Provided by publisher.
Identifiers: LCCN 2022019517 | ISBN 9781632933805 (paperback) | ISBN 9781611396737 (epub) | ISBN 9781632934499 (hardcover)
Subjects: LCSH: Lopez, Fernando (Fictitious character) | Murder--Investigation--Fiction. | Santa Fe (N.M.)--Fiction. | LCGFT: Detective and mystery fiction.
Classification: LCC PS3623.I58485 D43 2022 | DDC 813/.6--dc23/eng/20220516
LC record available at https://lccn.loc.gov/2022019517

WWW.SUNSTONEPRESS.COM
SUNSTONE PRESS / POST OFFICE BOX 2321 / SANTA FE, NM 87504-2321 /USA
(505) 988-4418

Dedicated to my longtime friend Alan Boye, who first introduced me to Canyon Road.

"The dead go fast."

—Samuel Beckett, *Endgame*

"Though justice be thy plea consider this, that in the course of justice none of us should see salvation."

—Shakespeare, *The Merchant of Venice*

PREFACE

Canyon Road has always been the center of artistic Santa Fe. When I lived on Canyon Road as a young man I found a collection of like-minded writers, musicians, and artists (painters, potters, sculptors, glass-blowers, you name it). We were all bohemians, living freely and probably a little too wildly for our own good. We had unlimited energy and the firm belief that art could change the world. Seems quaint now, I suppose, but it was a heady time.

Today, underneath the corporate glitz, you can still sense a bit of the old bohemian Canyon Road. Down one of the many colorful back alleys you might glimpse a ghost or two. Or walking up Canyon Road on a winter's day, with the turquoise sky above and the smell of burning piñon wood wafting in the cold air, you might feel a presence, just a hint of Canyon Road's colorful past.

I've always wanted to write about my time on Canyon Road, but until now I never found the right approach. In *The Dead Go Fast* I've tried to capture the spirit of the bohemians I knew back then. Don't get me wrong. This mystery is a work of fiction; its characters are not meant to be renderings of actual people. What I'm interested in is the spirit of bohemian Canyon Road, the spirit that infuses Jimmy Mackey and Ruby Montez and my other characters. I love them all, just as I love Canyon Road itself.

Jimmy Mackey's Hangover

Jimmy Mackey lay awake most of the night tormented by nightmares of his ex-wife Ruby and their tumultuous marriage. Two years later and the bitch still haunted his sleep as well as his waking life. When morning finally arrived he kicked out of his wet sheets and sat on the edge of the bed fighting a blinding headache. To make matters worse he was seriously dehydrated. He must have had too much to drink yesterday, even if he couldn't remember much about last night. He managed to stand up and shuffle into the bathroom, where he drank down a glass of water and popped an Oxy and a Tylenol for good measure. His image in the mirror startled him: unshaven, dark circles under red eyes, hair sticking up like goddamn porcupine quills. He couldn't remember the last time he shaved or washed his hair.

Searching for a quick fix, he stuck his head under the faucet and ran water over his head and let it splash onto the floor. Still dripping, he shuffled out of the bedroom that used to be a tack room in a carriage house before he bought and remodeled the building back in the 2000s. Whenever it rained you could still smell the goddamn horses once stabled there. The bedroom opened up on one large room where he'd installed an efficiency kitchen next to the bathroom and a small sitting area in the front of the building overlooking Canyon Road. He'd set aside most of the floor area for his open studio, where he painted day and night except when sleeping or drinking. Sometimes he even painted while drinking. Hell, he'd done some of his best work while drunk. Even his patron Blaine Rogers said as much and that fucker was hard to please. The studio reeked of paints and solvents, but he'd grown used to the biting smell.

He stopped first at the kitchen counter, cluttered with half a dozen glasses and an empty bottle of cheap tequila. How many people had been here last night? He couldn't remember a damn thing after he left El Farol. His memory did tricks on him these days, sometimes failing him altogether. Twenty years of heavy drinking had taken its toll. He wished he had the willpower to stick with AA, but after two failed stints, why bother? He couldn't fool himself into believing that a third try would be any different.

His hands shook as he filled a cup, popped in a cartridge, and hit the brew button on his Keurig coffeemaker. When the coffee was ready he took the cup over to his sitting area, which grew smaller every week as his painting took up more and more floor space. He sat on the sagging corduroy sofa and sipped his coffee, looking over the clutter of easels and half-finished paintings that crowded the center of the room near a picture window that provided the precious light he needed to paint. More paintings hung on the walls--pastel landscapes for the tourists and what he called Chopped Nudes for his soul. He liked the room just like this--a riot of color everywhere, even on the floor. Splotches of oil and acrylic paint splattered the tarps covering the floorboards. This morning his mixing table oozed with drying blues, blacks, and yellow oils from the painting he'd finished yesterday. Seeing the wet paint, he got up to make sure he'd properly put away his brushes in containers of turpentine and mineral spirits and breathed a sign of relief when he saw he had.

Outside the window he noticed a cop car pulling into the gravel parking lot between his studio and Essentia, the sex shop next door. He'd been spending way too much time at Essentia lately. He made a mental note to stay away from that fucking place. The last sex ointment he tried made his dick burn. Ruby screamed at him last week for using it during their latest frolic. "Owww...what is that, napalm?" she howled and kicked him out of her house. He made a mental note to stop having sex with his ex-wife.

While he watched, the cops parked behind a small white car that looked familiar. Two cops climbed out, one of them a big motherfucker, big as an NFL linebacker. The other one he recognized. A mean-spirited little prick named Ruiz who'd busted him for a number of bullshit offenses over the years. The two cops approached the white car with hands touching their holsters as if expecting trouble. What the fuck? Wait a minute, the car looked identical to Kim Martin's Beamer. Was she here last night? He couldn't remember.

He quickly finished his coffee and went back to his bedroom and pulled on a pair of white painter's pants and a blue T-shirt. Then he headed outside to deflect the trouble before it knocked on his door and bit him in the ass. Never let the cops inside if you can help it. You never knew what they could find––or plant. If they did trespass, he at least felt confident they wouldn't find his hidden stash under the floorboards in the bathroom.

The New Mexico sun nearly blinded him as he stepped outside. He shielded his eyes and walked down the wooden steps and across the gravel parking lot. He felt the Oxy kicking in as he moved in slow motion, floating easy-peasy, everything's groovy. "Hey officers. What's up? Is there a problem?"

Officer Ruiz studied him for a brief moment before speaking. "So, Mackey...you still live in this barn?"

"Uh, it's an old carriage house. I restored it myself."

The big gorilla glared at him. He looked like he could pick up a man and break him over his knee.

"So what's up?" Jimmy asked again.

Ruiz stepped forward into his face. "We got an APB on this vehicle an hour ago. The owner is missing. Her husband filed a Missing Person report. Do you know anything about it?"

Jimmy shook his head. "That looks like Kim Martin's car."

"It is Kim Martin's car. So you do know something about it. Like I said, the Mayor reported his wife missing this morning. What was she doing here?"

Jimmy bit his tongue. What were they trying to pin on him now? Better to shut up and say nothing.

"You didn't answer my question? What was she doing here?" Ruiz bellowed.

"I...I don't know. I can't remember. I mean, if she was here."

"You can't remember? How convenient."

"Maybe she stopped next door at Essentia."

"The sex shop? The Mayor's wife?"

That comment made him smile. He could tell them some juicy tales about Kim Martin, the former Kim Mendoza and before that the former Kim Young. "Yeah...she was a free spirit."

"So where were you last night?" Ruiz asked.

"Uh...I remember drinking at El Farol with some friends...then coming back here about midnight."

"Was Kim Martin with you?" Ruiz asked.

"No...it was my ex, Ruby Montez...and Blaine Rogers...and I think Rose Lucero."

"And these people will vouch for you?" Ruiz asked.

"Yeah they will. They weren't that drunk."

While they argued, the big guy searched the inside of the car and came back with a set of keys. He motioned for them to move back from the car and popped open the trunk. "Oh fuck!"

Jimmy caught a quick glimpse of the body before Ruiz shoved him away. Just a glimpse, but that and the smell were enough to make him retch. He turned his back and vomited on the gravel. When he finished emptying his stomach, he wiped his mouth with the back of his hand.

"Sorry. Too much tequila last night."

Jimmy avoided looking at the trunk and its grisly contents. The yellow dress covered with dark red blood. The ghastly white face with its eyes wide open, its mouth fixed in one final grimace. The knife embedded in the center of her chest. He felt sick again.

"I need to sit down," Jimmy said. "I think I'm gonna puke again."

The two officers ignored him, busy inspecting the body.

Jimmy went back inside his studio and collapsed on the sofa. Once again he tried to remember last night. Had Kim been at El Farol, after all? Had she come back here with him? Why couldn't he remember?

Moments later Ruiz and the big gorilla came up the steps into his studio. By the look on their faces he could tell he was in big trouble. They didn't bother with small talk.

"Okay, Mackey, where do you keep your silverware?"

"My what? My silverware? Why do you want to see that?"

Ruiz looked angry. He turned to the big guy. "He wants to know why we want to see his silverware."

The big cop reached down and grabbed him by his shirt collar and picked him up off the sofa with one hand. "Because the mayor's wife has a steak knife stuck in her ribcage, what do you think?"

Ruiz showed him a cellphone photo he'd taken of the knife handle protruding from Kim's chest. Dark wooden handle with three metal rivets.

"Okay, okay, let me go," Jimmy gasped. "The silverware is in a kitchen drawer...the small drawer under the counter top."

The big cop dropped him on the sofa and followed Ruiz to the kitchen counter. Ruiz opened the top drawer and rummaged through the drawer. Suddenly he stopped, smiling. "Well, well, take a look at this, Antonio," he said to his partner.

Ruiz held up a knife. Even from across the room he could see it was identical to the one in the photo. Dark wood, three metal rivets. Oh fuck!

Jimmy panicked, jumping up from the sofa. "Wait a minute! You can't pin this on me. I didn't kill her! Why would I kill Kim Martin? She was a good friend of mine, for fuck's sake!"

He had an urge to run for the door, but before he could move the big cop jumped him, pushing him down hard on the sofa and cuffing his hands behind his back while Ruiz read him his Miranda Rights.

Ruiz nodded. "Take him down to the station. I'll stay here and wait for forensics."

"Let me go! Please. I didn't kill her, you fucking assholes!" Jimmy screamed as the big cop drug him outside and stuffed him into the back seat of the cop car.

1

Detective Fernando Lopez adjusted his sunhat and continued picking ripe tomatoes and chiles from his vines. He was enjoying his first summer in years tending their garden. In previous years Estelle had done all the work. Thanks to a three-month medical leave from the Santa Fe Police Department he had time to do whatever the hell he wanted. Finally. He carefully picked each tomato and chile and placed them in the basket he carried. The chiles were just beginning to turn red, the perfect time to pick them. When the basket was full, he carried it over to the bench on their patio and sat down to rest.

He and Estelle had lived in their small adobe on Acequia Madre for over thirty years. He loved to sit out on the patio and relax under the cottonwoods. Their leaves were just beginning to turn yellow, the time of year that brought a morning chill to Santa Fe, a promise of cold weather ahead. He hadn't been this relaxed since he and Estelle had taken a two-week vacation to San Diego where all he did was lay on the beach and drink beer. This time he had three whole months of respite thanks to a cracked rib he'd suffered in a jeep accident at Chaco Canyon while chasing a looter. His own damned fault for driving lickety-split over the mesa and not seeing the arroyo ahead. He ended up at the bottom of the arroyo in a world of pain.

Now he had one month of medical leave remaining before he officially retired. He'd reached retirement age, so he could take his pension and be done with police work. He was tired of all the people with problems and tired of always butting heads with the Chief. They'd been at odds since the city hired Larry Stuart as Chief six years ago. To him, Stuart was an arrogant Anglo newcomer who had no understanding of the cultural and ethnic conflict that had defined Santa Fe for the past four hundred years. To Stuart, he was a Chicano with an attitude. They didn't like each other and they didn't trust each other. So maybe it was time to move on to fishing or gardening or whatever the hell people did when they retired.

While he brooded on retirement, he heard their front doorbell ring. Moments later Estelle came out to the back patio and said, "Fernando, you have a visitor."

He turned to find none other than Larry Stuart following Estelle. The coincidence was uncanny. Had his bad thoughts conjured the Chief out of thin air?

As Estelle left them, Stuart stood on the patio nervously looking at him. A short balding man with wire rimmed glasses, all of forty years old. Neither of them knew quite what to say, so they stared at each other for a long moment before Stuart spoke.

"So how are you feeling?"

"Better. The cracked rib is healing, and the doctors tell me the soreness in my shoulder will pass. Just takes time."

Stuart nodded. Another long moment of silence.

Fernando started to feel uncomfortable. Why didn't the man just say what he came to say?

Finally the Chief spoke. "Listen, Fernando...I know we don't always see eye to eye...that we've had our disagreements over the years. I'm sorry for that, for my part, because you're the best detective we have. Which is why I'm here."

"What do you mean?"

"I've come to ask you for a favor," Stuart said. "We have a dicey situation on our hands. This morning we got a call from the Mayor saying his wife, Kim, was missing. Antonio and Jerry found her car on Canyon Road parked in the lot between Essentia and Jimmy Mackey's studio. They found her body in the trunk of her car with a steak knife stuck in her ribcage. Looks like the steak knife came from a set they found in Mackey's kitchen, so they arrested Mackey and took him down to the station for booking. That's all I know at the moment."

Stuart raised his hand. "I know you and Mackey have a long history, and I know you're on medical leave pending retirement, but we really need you on this particular case."

"What's wrong with Armando or Manny?" Fernando asked.

Stuart shook his head. "Armando is too inexperienced...and Manny, you know Manny. He's too glib, always joking. This is a delicate situation with the Mayor and his wife, and we need someone with your experience. You're the best detective we have, Fernando. Everyone knows you're the best, including me. I've never questioned that from the first day I took this job. You have the respect around town that you'll need to deal with these people."

Fernando said nothing.

"Did you know the Mayor's wife?"

"Kim? Yes. I knew her when she was Kim Young and later when she was Kim Mendoza, long before she became Kim Martin."

"She was a wild one, I hear," Stuart said.

"That she was. I went to their wedding, the Martins. They seemed happy then, but later I started hearing stories about their problems."

"Their problems?"

"That he was possessive and abusive. That she was sleeping around. Rumors of a divorce."

"So you see my concern...we have a delicate situation, given who we're dealing with here," Stuart said. "Would you come back to active for this one case?"

Fernando considered. Against his better judgment, he said, "Okay, but just this one case."

Stuart smiled. "Thanks, Fernando. Much appreciated. Anything you need, just let me know."

"Is the forensic team still at Mackey's studio?"

"No, they finished a while ago. The body has been taken to the morgue and the car impounded. I expect they'll come back to the studio tomorrow to collect prints and DNA."

"Okay, then. I'll head down to the morgue."

Stuart came over to shake hands. "Thanks again, Fernando. I owe you one...big time."

He laughed. "Yes you do."

2

Fernando did indeed have a long history with Jimmy Mackey. Too long. An artist, a painter of some renown, Jimmy also happened to be a drunk prone to long binges and erratic, sometimes violent behavior. Over the years Fernando had had multiple encounters with the bad Jimmy, most of them triggered by alcohol-fueled arguments with his ex-wife Ruby or his brother after the brother had an affair with Ruby. Every so often Jimmy would get drunk at El Farol and start shooting up Canyon Road with an old Smith & Wessen he kept in his studio. He liked the sober Jimmy well enough, but the bad Jimmy was a mean drunk and a hard man to arrest, as he discovered two years ago when Jimmy turned his gun on him.

"Stop shooting, you crazy bastard!" he'd shouted at Jimmy out front of El Farol.

"I hate you!" Jimmy shouted back.

"I'm not your fucking brother," Fernando said, trying to wrestle the pistol out of Jimmy's hands when the gun exploded and blew off the tip of his little finger, after which Jimmy went to the drunk tank and he went to the ER.

Now this. He knew Jimmy and Kim Martin were friends if not occasional bed partners. Lovers would be an overstatement for the kind of coupling these two did.

The Chief was right, though. This would be a delicate investigation, given the people involved and their sexual habits.

He went inside to change his shirt and wash the dirt from his hands and face. The image staring back at him from the mirror no longer bore any resemblance to how he thought of himself. One glance, and then he hurried out of the bathroom away from this stranger with deep wrinkles, darkly tanned skin, and short-cropped gray hair. He put on a clean white shirt, grabbed what he needed from the hallway, and walked out the front door to his trusted Plymouth Acclaim, circa 2007. The car looked as good as it did back in 2007 thanks to a new paint job. The paint job cost more than the car's *Blue Book* value, but he had no choice after some sonofabitch scratched DEAD MAN on the driver's side door.

He followed the Paseo to St. Francis and then drove to the Christus St. Vincent Medical Center on St. Michael's Drive. He took the main elevator down to the basement where a cold, tiled corridor off-limits to the public directed him to the morgue. Miguel and Teresa greeted him in the front office, having just finished their autopsy of Kim Martin.

"Didn't expect to see you here," Miguel said, a small wiry man wearing scrubs. "What happened to your medical leave? I thought you were retiring."

"Chief asked me to come back for the Martin case. It's kind of delicate, if you know what I mean."

Miguel laughed. "Yeah. I would say so...the Mayor's wife."

Fernando grunted. "Have you finished the autopsy?"

"Just finished, take a look for yourself," Teresa said, a heavy-set young woman wearing scrubs and a cap over her long dark hair.

She led him into the dimly-lit dissection room where red lights blinked on the wall panel and somewhere a machine whirred and beeped. Then he saw the body of Kim Martin on the table--white, as white as porcelain, except for the Y-incision and the heavy stitches that criss-crossed her chest. Even in death, disfigured on the autopsy table, she was a real knockout. Her short blond hair made her look younger than her years, as did the slender curve of her hips. He couldn't help but notice the Mohawk tuft of hair above her vagina.

"You can see the wound in the center of her chest, next to the stitches. Doesn't look like much, but the knife blade nicked the aortic artery and she bled to death."

Fernando nodded, looking at the wound.

Teresa pointed to a plastic bag on the counter. "There's the knife. It has a five-inch blade, more than enough to do the deed."

"Prints?"

Teresa shook her head. "It's clean. Whoever killed her either wore gloves or wiped it clean."

Fernando pointed to a bruise on Kim's face. "What's this?"

"Looks like someone hit her...or maybe she fell after she was stabbed."

Miguel joined them at the table. "Take a look at her BMW when you get a chance. We found more blood on the front seat and steering wheel than in the trunk, where the body was discovered. That means she bled to death either driving to Mackey's studio...or trying to drive away from it. Later someone placed the body in the trunk, probably the murderer."

Fernando thought about this for a moment. "How much time would she have had before bleeding out? If she'd been stabbed elsewhere I don't see how she could have driven all the way up Canyon Road to Mackey's studio."

Miguel turned to Teresa. "What do you think?"

She shook her head. "Hard to know. The knife blade didn't sever the aortic artery altogether...but it did puncture it."

"Probably more likely that she was stabbed at Mackey's studio, unless she managed to compress the wound somehow while driving," Miguel added.

Fernando nodded. "What else did you find in the car?"

"Let me show you," Miguel said.

Fernando followed them back to the office where Miguel put on a fresh pair of latex gloves and produced a cardboard container. He held up a small handgun. "This was in the glove compartment."

Fernando took a closer look. "Guardian .25 NAA. Nice little pistol. But why would Kim need a gun?"

Miguel ignored his question and continued. "We found this pearl earring in the trunk and these two paper receipts stuck in one of the front coffee cup holders. One's a receipt from Tiny's Lounge and the other a print-out of a reservation at the Inn on the Alameda."

Fernando put on latex gloves and examined the documents himself. They were both dated yesterday. The Tiny's receipt totaled over $50 in drinks for two people. The Inn on the Alameda's reservation totaled $325 for a one-night stay for one person. He read aloud the name on the receipt: "Kim Young."

"Yeah, she used her maiden name," Teresa said. "Some hanky-panky going on there?"

Fernando grunted. "What about the earring? Was she wearing a match on one of her ears?"

"No, she came in without earrings or jewelry of any kind, except a watch, which we have with her clothing."

"Okay, thanks. I'll check out the car and then take a look around the house."

"We'll be back at the house tomorrow morning dusting and collecting," Teresa said. "We didn't have time to finish today."

"Maybe I'll join you," Fernando said and walked out of the office and into the long corridor to the elevator.

Outside he found his car in the parking lot and got back on St. Francis Drive. He knew he had to question both Jimmy Mackey and Mayor Joe Martin soon if not sooner, but he dreaded both interviews, especially Joe Martin's. The Mayor would be damn embarrassed by all this, for obvious reasons. And before he talked to either of them he wanted to take a look at the impounded car and especially Jimmy's house, just to get the lay of the land. He decided to stop first at the Police Impound Lot on Siler Road and then drive up to Jimmy's studio on Canyon Road.

Canyon Road had been the center of Santa Fe's artistic scene for over a hundred years, the home of artists, bohemians, and assorted ne'er-do-wells. He had mixed feelings about getting involved with that crowd.

3

Stopping by the impound lot turned out to be a waste of time. Miguel and Teresa had picked the car clean. One thing that did surprise Fernando was the amount of dried blood in the front cabin, including on the steering wheel. Hard to imagine Kim driving very far while bleeding like that. Whoever stuck a knife in her chest had to have done it at the studio.

Sergeant Antonio Blake met him at Jimmy's studio with the key to the front door. He saw the big man waiting impatiently on the wooden porch when he pulled into the parking lot. An ex-Marine who stood six feet, seven inches tall and weighed 280 pounds, Antonio was considered the SFPD's enforcer. He had the physical presence and temperament to intimidate anyone foolish enough to cross him.

"Good to see you again, Fernando," Antonio said as he walked to the porch. "What happened with your medical leave? You missed us so much you couldn't stay away?"

Fernando laughed. "Something like that. The Chief came over this morning and asked me to take over this investigation as a personal favor to him. Because of the people involved."

"Good thing. Manny and his wisecracks, he's gonna piss off the Chief one of these days and get his ass fired," Antonio said. "This thing with the mayor is way beyond his capability."

He grunted his agreement while Antonio opened the front door. He'd been here more times than he cared to remember––delivering citations, summons, arrest orders, you name it. Each time he paid Jimmy a visit his gallery looked more congested. He could hardly find a path through the studio to the back bedroom. Paintings were hanging and stacked along the walls, as well as propped up in easels. Big, bright canvasses with thick brushstrokes and globs of paint for emphasis or whatever the hell globs of paint are supposed to accomplish. The tourists bought his landscapes, but around town Jimmy was primarily known for his Chopped Nudes series. That is, abstract paintings of women with legs growing out of their heads and arms sticking out of their wazoos. His supporters likened him to Picasso. His detractors called him a mere imitator without an original idea in his head.

The cramped sitting area in the front of the studio showed signs of a party last night. He saw paper cups and glasses and ashtrays stuffed with cigarette butts. Same with the kitchen counter, where an empty, overturned bottle of tequila lay beside a plate of diced limes. He made a mental note that the dicing knife was nowhere to be seen. The murder weapon?

Antonio followed him into the small bedroom in back, barely large enough to contain a queen-size bed and dresser. He saw sheets and a bedspread pulled halfway off the bed and twisted in knots. Dirty clothes littered the floor near the wall. On a small bedside table he found a wineglass half filled with red wine and a torn condom wrapper empty now.

"Take a look at this," Antonio said from the other side of the bed.

He walked around behind him and saw a woman's hairbrush and compact on the floor. When he bent down to take a closer look, he also found a scattering of coins on the floor.

"Purse must have fallen on the floor," Antonio said.

"Yeah...and not Kim Martin's. The brush is matted with long black hair. Kim's hair is blond."

Fernando stood up and stretched his back. "Okay. Tell Miguel and Teresa to process the glasses and the cigarettes and everything on the floor here. Let's get the prints and the DNA as soon as possible."

"Will do."

They made their way back through the studio to the front door. Antonio locked up and turned to him. "So what do you think?"

Fernando shrugged. "Clearly there were several people here last night. We'll have to identify those people."

"Mackey said he couldn't remember. What bullshit."

"Well, I'm hoping you can spend a little time with him this afternoon," Fernando said. "Maybe refresh his memory."

Antonio smiled.

"I'll meet you down at the station. I want to pay Essentia a visit and see if they saw anything unusual. On your way why don't you stop at El Farol and ask what they remember about Jimmy last night, who he was with, that sort of thing."

Antonio saluted and headed for his cruiser.

Fernando walked across the parking lot to the front entrance of Essentia, a ramshackle adobe painted pink with dark red trim and stained glass windows. The windows reflected the sunlight and made it seem like the building was glowing from the inside like an alien spacecraft, very New Age looking. He knew the owners, Paul and June Bryan, from the Chaco Canyon investigation that landed him on medical leave earlier that summer. They sold a variety of sex toys, everything from whips and masks to dildos of every size, shape, and color. Not only sex toys, but what they called 'medicinals.' That included lubricants, oils and unguents to juice the body, as well as stimulants like eucalyptus and ylang ylang to juice the libido. Or so they said.

He nearly gagged when he stepped into a front room filled with incense. Clouds of rancid smoke snaked up to the ceiling, glowing in the light from the stained glass windows. Through the smoke he saw June standing behind the front counter, a small mousy woman with short blue hair who advertised herself as a masseuse and a karmic healer, whatever that meant. She'd worn tights or leotards every time he'd seen her. Today was no different.

"Detective Lopez...fancy seeing you again so soon," she said as he approached the counter.

"Seems there was some trouble up here last night."

"Yeah, we talked to the two policemen this morning," June said. "They told us Kim Martin was murdered."

Fernando nodded. "That's why I'm here. Did you see or hear anything over at Jimmy Mackey's studio last night that might help us find out what happened?"

"Nothing out of the ordinary," she said, laughing. "It's usually pretty noisy over there. Jimmy gets wild when he drinks, and his friends aren't much better. Last night they woke me up about midnight. I heard them coming up from El Farol singing and roughhousing. Paul almost went outside to tell them to shut up, but I told him not to go. When he's like that, Jimmy is liable to do anything. He's even shot up the street a couple of times since we've been here. Both times he ended up in jail."

This time Fernando was the one who laughed. "Yes he did. And that's where he is now."

"You think Jimmy murdered Kim Martin?"

He ignored her question. "How do you know they were coming up from El Farol? Were you there earlier?"

"No, but that's where they always drink, the Canyon Road crowd," she said.

Fernando nodded. "You say they woke you up. Jimmy and how many others?"

"Well, I looked out our bedroom window and saw the group coming up the street. It was dark, so I can't say for sure, but there must have been four or five of them."

"So three or four people in addition to Jimmy," Fernando said.

"I think so."

"Did you recognize any of their voices?"

"I heard Ruby's voice, Jimmy's ex-wife. She and Jimmy were screaming at each other, as usual. I'm not sure about the other voices. One might have been Blaine Rogers. He was a big guy."

Fernando looked at her. "Blaine?"

"He owns the gallery that sells Jimmy's paintings. Picasso and Company."

Fernando nodded. "Did you know Kim Martin?"

"Not well. She came over to Jimmy's a lot, sometimes with Rose Lucero...you know, the arts critic at the *Independent*? And sometimes she stopped in here to buy our products."

Fernando had never heard of Rose Lucero. The others he knew. "Really? What did Kim buy? I'm curious."

She looked at him askance. "I shouldn't really say, but I guess it doesn't matter now that she's dead. She mostly bought our medicinals, stimulants and other performance enhancers."

"For the people she slept with--like Jimmy?"

She shrugged. "Could be. Or maybe they were for her husband. He had some sort of problem performing. I think that's one of the reasons she slept around."

When Fernando didn't respond, she continued. "They must have had an open marriage."

"Apparently so. Okay. One more question. Was Kim one of the people you saw walking up Canyon Road?"

"No, she wasn't with them. I didn't see her car in the parking lot until this morning."

"So she came in the middle of the night," Fernando said.

"Yes...as she always did.

He nodded. "Here's my card. If you can think of anything else, give me a call."

4

The dispatcher, Linda Stephens, greeted him with a big smile as he walked into the Washington Avenue Station. She shook her head. "Well, well, if it isn't Fernando Lopez himself. I thought you were on medical leave--laid up in rehab and on your way to retirement. What brings you back from the dead?"

He laughed. "Jimmy Mackey."

"Oh God. You agreed to take the Mackey case?" She rolled her eyes in mock horror.

He loved Linda's sense of humor. An old hippie with long gray hair and a wicked sense of humor, she'd moved down to Santa Fe from Taos in the late 1970s after becoming disillusioned with living in the New Buffalo commune. He'd had a brief affair with Linda many years ago, his only indiscretion in the forty years he'd been married to Estelle. They'd broken it off to save their friendship...as well as his marriage.

"Wait a minute. Isn't Jimmy the drunk who shot you?" Linda asked.

"That's him. He's a real sweetheart."

She gave him a serious look and whispered. "Be careful, Fernando. This involves the Mayor and his wife."

"So everyone says."

Fernando turned and walked down the long hall to his office, stale and dusty after being vacant for over a month. He raised the blinds and opened the window to let in some fresh air, which helped some. His desk was cluttered with loose papers and folders and empty coffee cups. He filed some of the crap in his wastebasket and ignored the rest. Now what? He decided to make a list of all the people he needed to question, so he took out his pocket notebook and started scribbling names. Before long he had a long list, starting with the Mayor and ending with Jimmy. Might as well start with the one he dreaded the most.

Just then Antonio appeared in the doorway, interrupting his thoughts. The big man stepped into his office and sat in the chair across from his desk. "Okay, I stopped at El Farol and spoke with the bartender and one of the servers," Antonio said. "Both said Jimmy and three of his pals came in about eight last night and didn't leave until nearly midnight. Apparently all of them were drunk and obnoxious and were asked to leave finally after one of them spilled a pitcher of beer on their table. They refused to leave and had to be escorted out by Bill, the night bartender. One of them punched Bill on the way out, but no one knows who since everyone was pushing and shoving. Sounds like it was quite a scene."

"Did you get their names?"

Antonio nodded. "Yeah, Jimmy's ex-wife Ruby. Rose Lucero, the arts reporter for the *Independent*. And Blaine Rogers, who owns the gallery where Jimmy's paintings are sold."

"Yeah. Picasso and Company."

Antonio laughed. "As if."

"So tell me this, did you get a chance to spend some time with Jimmy and refresh his memory?" Fernando asked.

"Hah! They let him go. They released him."

"What are you talking about?"

"The District Attorney wants hard evidence, prints or DNA. The murder weapon was clean. He says the knife coming from Jimmy's studio isn't enough to bring charges. There were other people at the party." Antonio threw up his hands.

The news disappointed but didn't surprise Fernando. Steve Chabot was known as a stickler for detail. He wanted the goods before bringing charges. Otherwise everyone in the department looked foolish.

Antonio continued. "Yeah, and we got bigger problems. Raoul Garcia is representing Jimmy. He's saying whatever evidence we have was illegally obtained because we didn't have a subpoena to enter Jimmy's studio. You know Raoul, he's raising hell and crying police brutality. Next he'll be saying Jimmy is a political prisoner."

Fernando's spirits sank. Unfortunately, he did know Raoul. He remembered him as a fiery young lawyer who represented radical Chicano leaders and organizations like La Raza as far back as the late seventies. He called his clients "political prisoners," men and women charged with everything from growing pot to making armed raids on county courthouses. Raoul built a reputation for taking on the system every chance he got and winning more times than he lost.

Not an easy task for an aggressive, smart-ass Chicano lawyer who all the Anglos in the judicial system hated. But times had changed, and so had Raoul and his clientele. Instead of fire-bombing courthouses, the young Chicanos he represented now shot each other in gangs over territory or drugs. And Raoul had changed, too. He continued to service his rabble-rousers, but he also did a lucrative trade in real estate development and celebrity lawsuits, having become one of the premier trial lawyers in all of northern New Mexico. There wasn't a lawyer or district attorney in the state who didn't fear coming up against Raoul.

More trouble. As if he didn't have enough already.

"So what do you want me to do?"

Fernando glanced at his notebook. "Why don't you take Rose Lucero and Blaine Rogers. I'll take the Mayor and Ruby."

Antonio laughed. "Good luck with that. I don't know whose worse, Joe Martin or Ruby."

5

The Mayor had been expecting his call and had cancelled all afternoon appointments. Fernando took his time walking to city hall, debating how to approach the interview. He found the Mayor waiting outside his office door, eager to talk. With him stood his personal bodyguard Al Monroe. He could tell by the look on Martin's face that he was nervous, worried. About what, he intended to find out. "Mr. Mayor," he said and shook hands.

"Fernando, please come in," Martin said, leading the way into his office. A small balding man with traces of gray hair, he wore his usual Santa Fe Chic: jeans, concho belt, and turquoise bolo tie. Every outsider who wanted to look like a bonafide Santa Fean wore the same costume. It drove him crazy.

The Mayor's office proved quite a contrast to his dark, dreary office back at the station. For one thing the Mayor had real furniture: leather chairs and sofa and a wooden desk and lo and behold an actual rug on the floor. Even shelves of kachinas and Pueblo pottery. Not the metal furniture and bare linoleum floor he lived with. For another thing the bay window behind the Mayor's desk bathed the entire room in a warm glow. Sunny. Cheerful.

They sat in leather chairs facing each other.

"I'm sorry for your loss," Fernando began.

"No, it's...I might as well be frank with you. My wife and I were separated and in the midst of a divorce. She'd been staying with friends and rarely spent the night at our house. You might have heard, she was something of a free spirit."

"Did she come home last night?"

The mayor frowned. "No, she didn't come home. I didn't see her at all yesterday."

"Where were you last night?" Fernando asked.

"Home. I was working on the agenda for the upcoming City Council meeting."

"Can anyone verify that?"

"No, but you don't think–"

Fernando raised his hand. "Just routine questions. They'll want to search your house. When something like this happens, it's usually a family member. You know how it goes."

Martin looked away, attempting to hide his irritation.

"Do you know anyone who would want to harm your wife?" Fernando asked.

"Besides me, you mean?" It was meant as a joke, but it fell flat.

Fernando ignored the joke. "Anyone she had argued with or who had threatened her recently?"

"Not really," the Mayor said. "Although she was the kind of person who rubbed a lot of people the wrong way, if you know what I mean. She was a force of nature. Very headstrong. She did what she wanted to do and to hell with the consequences."

"What exactly are you saying?" Fernando asked.

"Well, let's just say she had a difficult time living up to her marriage vows," Martin began and then paused for a moment to find the right words. "What I mean is that she slept around, always had. During all of her marriages. She was the kind of person who shouldn't be married."

"Do you have any idea where she was last night…or who she was with?" Fernando asked.

"None."

"We found a print-out of a reservation for last night at the Inn on the Alameda. But it appears she never made it there."

"Well, then, she probably had a date for another tryst with someone at the inn," Martin said.

"Did the two of you ever have violent arguments?"

"Jesus…I suppose we had shouting matches. Doesn't every couple? But none that ever became violent. I mean I never physically abused her, if that's what you're getting at."

Fernando shook his head. "No, I'm just covering all the bases. SOP."

That seemed to satisfy Martin.

"But you must have had some marital problems, since the two of you were divorcing."

"Sure, like any married couple," Martin said. "For us...well, Kim was hyper sexual, as you've probably heard. She had an enormous libido, which quite frankly I couldn't satisfy. I'm five years older, and as my life has gotten busier I just don't have the time or the energy I once had for those matters."

Fernando thought for a moment. "So who had she been spending time with? Who were her friends?"

"Kim? She was always drawn to the bohemian types. Artists like Jimmy Mackey and his ex-wife Ruby Montez. She liked to hang out with them, they made her feel artistic. And there was this big guy, Blaine, who owned the gallery that sold Jimmy's paintings."

"Blaine Rogers," Fernando said.

"Yes, that's him. Big guy with rough manners. A brute, really. I don't know what she saw in him."

"You mean she was having an affair with him?" Fernando asked.

"I don't know for sure. Maybe. Probably."

"Can you think of anyone else in that group."

"No one in particular, but there were others who hung out at the gallery...or the pottery co-op that Ruby Montez owns."

Fernando waited because he sensed that Martin had something else he wanted to say.

"Anything else you care to add?"

Martin shook his head. "Just this. Find whoever did this. We had our differences, but she didn't deserve to die like that. Okay?"

"We'll find the murderer," Fernando said, standing.

The Mayor watched him walk out of the office and down the hallway.

Fernando felt a sense of relief when he stepped outside into the sunshine. The interview had gone better than he anticipated, even though Martin hadn't told him much he didn't already know.

Instead of going to his office he walked to his car and drove up Marcy to the Paseo and around to East Alameda Street. Once through the light he turned sharply to the left and pulled into the tiny parking lot of the Inn on the Alameda. Inside the lobby he found a young man behind the front counter. He identified himself and showed his badge.

"I need to check on someone who rented a room last night, a blond woman named Kim Martin."

The young man went to his computer and hit a few keys. Then he looked up.

"Oh yeah, she was the woman who never showed up. This morning housekeeping found the room hadn't been occupied."

"So Kim made the reservation?"

"Yeah, she used her credit card."

"For one person or two?" Fernando asked.

The young man checked the computer screen. "One guest."

"Are you sure?"

"That's what she typed on the reservation...although she asked for two queen beds."

"Why would she ask for two beds if she were planning on being alone?" Fernando asked.

The young man shrugged. "Beats me."

He thanked the clerk and headed for the door, thinking he might know who killed Kim if he knew the identity of whoever Kim was expecting in that other bed.

6

Over dinner Fernando and Estelle swapped stories about their days. She told him about her work for the Saint Francis Outreach Program, a religious nonprofit that helped immigrants find food and shelter and legal services in Santa Fe. He told her about Kim Martin and his interview with the Mayor. These quiet moments with Estelle always made him feel lucky. They had done well together, especially considering how young they were when they married, Estelle only nineteen and him twenty, high school sweethearts. But they had been good for each other, as sentimental as that sounded. He'd never for one moment regretted their youthful decision to marry and spend their lives together.

For the first few years of their marriage he worked part-time at Johnson's Lumber Yard and took classes at the University of New Mexico, majoring in Criminal Justice. When Flavia was born, their first child, he dropped out of UNM and entered the Santa Fe Police Academy. Not only did he need a full-time job to support the family, he decided that instead of studying Criminal Justice he would rather work in the field. Those early years on the SFPD were the hardest, because back then he and the other young Chicanos were treated like second-class citizens. Ironic, since many of them were from Santa Fe's oldest families. But he learned to swallow his pride and hold his tongue. He learned to accept the shit assignments.

Yes, he had paid his dues. Big time.

After dinner he washed the dishes and put them away. Then they made tea and went out on the back patio to enjoy the warm evening, with fireflies sparkling in the cottonwoods along the acequia and a three-quarters moon hanging in the night sky. The smell of a Santa Fe autumn was in the air tonight, that whiff of piñon and ponderosa pine that he so loved. Not many people knew that Santa Fe was located at an altitude of 7,200 feet, so there was always that scent of mountain pine in the air.

Eventually Estelle went back inside to watch television or listen to the music on KUNM, her favorite ways to relax in the evening. He stayed outside on the patio for a while, ruminating on how he always felt a sense of relief when he stepped inside their small adobe, where they had lived since early in their marriage. Stress from work seemed to melt away the instant he walked through their front door.

Their house might be small by today's standards, but it had been big enough to raise two children back in his day, before the rich Anglos from New York and Los Angeles moved to Santa Fe and remodeled the old adobes on streets like Acequia Madre into million-dollar mansions. He took great pride in the fact that he had preserved the original look of his adobe, built in the 1920s. Secretly it gave him a great deal of pleasure to know that their house had become something of an eyesore to many of his wealthy neighbors

He was deep in thought when his cell phone rang.

"Detective Lopez?"

He couldn't quite place the woman's voice.

"This is June Bryan...from Essentia. I think there's more trouble at Jimmy Mackey's studio. I wanted to let you know right away. Sounds like Jimmy and someone else are fighting. We heard screaming and shouting and things being smashed over there. I'm worried that someone has been seriously injured, because it's suddenly all quiet now."

"Were the voices male or female?" Fernando asked.

"Both of them were male. I recognized Jimmy. The other might be Blaine Rogers. He has a loud booming voice. Always sounds angry."

"Did you see anyone go into the studio?"

"Just Jimmy when he came home this afternoon," June said.

Fernando sighed. "Okay, I'm on my way."

He didn't bother to tell Estelle where he was going, not wanting to worry her. She'd be in bed soon anyway. He strapped on his holster with its .41 Magnum Smith & Wessen and stepped out into the driveway. The moon overhead provided enough light for him to walk to his car. He hit the clutch and eased his gear-shift into neutral, letting the Plymouth roll down to the end of the driveway. Then he fired the engine and drove slowly, quietly down Acequia Madre so as to not alert Estelle.

Once on Canyon Road he decided to park a couple of blocks below Jimmy's studio and walk the rest of the way. Walking would give him the element of surprise as he approached. He listened for shouting or any indication of an argument ahead but heard nothing but the cicadas in the cottonwoods down on Alameda. He'd walked about halfway when he heard the roar of a car engine and the sound of tires spinning on loose gravel. Suddenly a car came careening out of the parking lot between Essentia and Jimmy's studio spraying gravel everywhere.

He froze, blinded by the car's headlights as it swerved from one side of the road to the other. He had just enough time to shout and then dive into the ditch alongside Canyon Road. He rolled down a small hill smack-dab into a prickly pear cactus. Cursing, he extracted himself from the prickly pear and scrambled up the embankment. From there he watched the car race down Canyon Road and turn right on the Paseo. Everything happened so fast he didn't get a good look at the driver of the car. Or notice if anyone else was in the car.

Still cursing, he spent a few minutes picking cactus needles out of his left shoulder and arm. It hurt like hell every time he extracted one of the sharp spines. Trying to ignore the pain, he hurried up to the studio to check on Jimmy. He crossed the dark parking lot and climbed the steps to Jimmy's porch. The front door hung open, revealing a dark interior. He reached inside the doorway and felt along the wall until he found the light switch. Then he tripped the switch and stood back, instantly flooding the studio with a sickly yellow light.

What he saw puzzled him—a sea of broken glass and furniture. Someone had picked up a small side-table and smashed it on the kitchen sink, showering the kitchen counters and floor with wooden shards and splinters. Several of Jimmy's easels had been knocked over and tubes of paint scattered on the floor. He found traces of blood on one wall. In the bedroom he found clothes thrown on the bed and a bloody washcloth in the bathroom sink.

June was right. It looked like someone had taken a beating, most likely Jimmy, since he was a foot shorter and fifty pounds lighter than Blaine. If Blaine had been the person Jimmy quarreled with.

He spotted an open cabinet across the room that turned out to be Jimmy's liquor cabinet. Only a nearly empty bottle of gin and an old, sticky bottle of Kahlua remained. Someone had cleaned out the cabinet.

When he left he locked and closed the front door behind him. He walked into the parking lot and looked around, noticing the door to the garage behind the studio was also open. Not a good sign. Was the intruder still on the premises?

He took out his revolver and crept slowly down the hill toward the garage. He regretted not bringing a flashlight with him, big mistake. As he came closer he saw the garage was empty. Jimmy's car, a green Subaru Outback, was gone. That meant either Jimmy or his assailant had driven the car that nearly flattened him on Canyon Road a few minutes earlier.

He decided to check out the garage before leaving. He needed light, so he felt around the wall inside the door until he found a light switch. When he flipped the switch he saw a workbench in the back of the building. Tools of all kinds littered the bench and hung from the wall above. One of the cabinets under the bench had been opened revealing an empty shelf. He walked over and opened the other cabinets and found an assortment of carpentry tools and tool sets on each of the other shelves. He figured someone must have opened the one cabinet and taken out whatever tools were stored there.

So someone, either Jimmy or his attacker, had grabbed a supply of liquor and a bunch of tools and taken off. But why? Where the hell were they going?

7

Fernando listened to the recorded message for the third time that morning. "You've reached Ruby Montez. You can leave a message but why bother? Chances are I won't call you back anyway."

Ruby wore her bad attitude with pride. To her, it was a badge of honor. Her in-your-face personality put off many people but had made her a force in Santa Fe politics for over two decades. A potter by trade, Ruby had risen through the ranks of *La Raza* to become the most progressive member of City Council ever. Back in the 1990s she fought tooth and nail with all the greedy developers who wanted to turn downtown Santa Fe into one big shopping mall. She led rallies, marches, protests, sit-ins, and if you believed the rumors, a fire-bombing or two.

She lost, of course. The developers and the Sotheby's crowd turned Santa Fe into Disneyland Southwest. The tide of gentrification sweeping over Santa Fe during those years hollowed out the city. Gone were most of the people whose families had lived in Santa Fe for generations. Increasingly higher home values and property taxes priced out all who couldn't afford the million dollar homes. After two tumultuous terms on City Council lecturing, berating, cajoling, and threatening the other members, she said 'fuck it' and retired to the pottery co-op she owned and ran with a number of other potters, most of them women.

Still she refused to be silenced. She made it a point to attend most Council meetings and give the members a piece of her mind. Every one of them feared Ruby's tirades. Occasionally her anger would get the better of her language and she would be asked to leave. Once a few years back City Council banned her for the year, but her lawyer, Raoul Garcia, sued their asses and got her reinstated in her front row seat staring down the Council.

He and Ruby had always been friendly, probably because he felt the same way about gentrification. They remained friends even after she married Jimmy Mackey who had been a thorn in his side for years. Ruby's marriage to Jimmy lasted less than a year, which was longer than most of their friends thought it would last. They fought constantly, even in public, contributing to Jimmy's drinking problem and Ruby's bad attitude. Since their divorce they'd remained friendly combatants, seeming to enjoy the time they spent together bickering and under the sheets humping. They remained ex-spouses with benefits.

This morning, since Jimmy had disappeared, he wanted to hear Ruby's account of the night Kim Martin was murdered. He tried telephoning once more and then decided to drive down to her pottery co-op at the Railyard. The day was slipping away fast. He needed something to tell the Chief at their meeting later today. Some semblance of progress in the investigation.

He took the Paseo to the Railyard and parked on the street. He walked into the refurbished warehouse divided now into work-stations for the potters. He spotted Ruby hunched over her wheel toward the rear of the building near a row of kilns. She wore her usual jeans and blue work shirt with a red bandana tied around her long curly black hair. As he came closer he saw her face and clothing were streaked with the gray clay that oozed between her fingers as her creation spun on the wheel.

Sitting beside Ruby was none other than Rose Lucero, the arts reporter for the *Independent*. A slender woman with short-cropped hair and tattoos running down both arms, she wore a tight black skirt and white blouse.

Ruby smiled. "Fernando. *Que pasa*? Where you been?"

"On medical leave, waiting to retire. I managed to get myself injured in a jeep accident at Chaco Canyon."

"You? You don't drive fast enough to get in an accident. You drive like an old man."

He laughed. "Nice to see you too, Ruby. I've missed your insults."

"You know I'm only kidding, bro. I love you." She turned off her wheel and wiped her hands on her jeans.

"We go back a long way, it's true," he said.

"Twenty years or more, back when I was on Council."

"Yeah, I had a crush on you...but you were even more inapproachable than you are now."

"Hah! Everybody had a crush on me back then. They all wanted to get in my pants. That's why I became a bitch in my old age."

Fernando laughed.

"Let me guess. You're here to ask what I know about the murder at Jimmy's studio. I can save you the trouble. *Nada*."

"You were there with him, yes?"

"Yeah, a bunch of us had a few drinks at El Farol, the usual Canyon Road group," Ruby said. "Then we walked up to the studio, must have been about midnight. Jimmy and I were fighting about all the money he owes me. He claimed to be broke, so I called him a fucking asshole and left right away. Rose and Blaine stayed for a while after I left. I don't know how long they could have put up with Jimmy. He was drunk and obnoxious as usual."

Rose nodded. "I stayed for one drink. Then Jimmy and Blaine started arguing about business, so I just left." She spoke with her tight little mouth closed, like a ventriloquist.

"What do you mean arguing about business?"

"They always argued about business," Ruby added. "Jimmy wanted Blaine to show more of his work at the gallery--Blaine wanted Jimmy to give him better work instead of all the tourist shit."

Fernando turned to Rose. "Did their argument turn violent?"

"Not while I was there, but I only stayed for one drink."

"Did either of you see Kim Martin there that night?"

Both women shook their heads.

"No, the parking lot was empty when I left," Ruby said. "She always parked next to the porch."

"So she came there frequently?" Fernando asked.

"Yeah, she and Jimmy were tight."

"Do you think Jimmy would ever harm her?"

"Jimmy? No way! He's a drunk, not a murderer," Ruby said.

"Hah!" Fernando laughed. "Tell that to the people he's tried to shoot, including me."

"Well...he does get crazy when he's drunk, but he's not a murderer. I know Jimmy better than anyone."

"Still, he says he doesn't remember what happened, so who knows?" Fernando said.

Ruby glared at him. “Listen, everyone there that night had been fucking Kim. Boys and girls. We loved her. No one in that group would ever harm her.”

Rose blushed. She looked down, avoiding his eyes. Then she excused herself and went to the restroom.

Fernando watched her walk away. “What’s wrong with her?”

“Nothing. She’s just young. She gets embarrassed easily.”

“So I see.”

“You gotta understand,” Ruby said. “Kim was a goddess. She was Aphrodite and Venus in one delicious body. Watching her undress could make you crazy. The way she moved--like a cat. You have no idea, my friend.”

“But someone did kill her,” Fernando added.

“Yeah, probably her husband, our lame-ass mayor. You know as well as I do that family members are guilty in most of these cases. Plus, she was divorcing him. She was sleeping around and everyone in Santa Fe knew it. That had to piss him off big time.”

Fernando threw open his arms, conceding. “You might be right. He certainly had the motive.”

“Not to mention that he was jealous and possessive, according to Kim. He accosted her and Jimmy when he saw the two of them together at the Shed last week.”

“What do you mean accosted?” Fernando asked.

“He yelled at them and threatened Jimmy. Right in front of a room-full of people.”

Fernando paused for a moment and then brought the conversation back to Jimmy. “So have you heard from Jimmy since that night?”

Ruby laughed. “No. I probably won’t. He knows I want the money he owes me.”

“The reason I ask is because he seems to have disappeared.”

“What do you mean?” Ruby asked.

“I received a call from Essentia last night about a disturbance at the studio. When I got there I found a room full of busted furniture and blood smeared on the walls and no Jimmy.”

Ruby looked worried. “Maybe the murderer came back to finish the job. Like I said, Joe Martin is a jealous man.”

“Maybe so. But walking in I was nearly run over by a car speeding away from the studio. The driver could have been either Jimmy or whoever he was fighting with. If it was Jimmy, where might he go to hide out for a while?"

"My house...I suppose."

Fernando frowned. "But you said you haven't seen Jimmy. If he didn't come to your house last night, where might he have gone?"

Ruby thought for a long moment. "Maybe Blaine's house. They're partners. Blaine sells pretty much all of Jimmy's paintings at his gallery. Other than that, I can't imagine."

"Doesn't he have any other drinking buddies?" Fernando asked.

"Well, the regulars at El Farol, especially Dave Stein and Wayne Fontenot. They're both painters and heavy drinkers," she added, laughing. "But I don't know. They both live in hovels that make Jimmy's studio look like a palace."

He wrote down the names in his notebook and then asked, "Jimmy still drives that old Subaru, yes?"

"Yeah, he drives an old Outback, one of those green L.L. Bean models they made back in the nineties or the two thousands, whenever."

"Okay. Thanks."

Ruby smiled. "Don't be a stranger, Fernando."

"Here's a card. If you hear from Jimmy, let me know." He looked around for Rose but didn't see her anywhere in the Co-op.

Ruby waved as he walked out of the warehouse to the parking lot. His cell phone rang just as he reached his car.

He recognized Antonio's voice. "Fernando, I'm at Blaine Rogers' gallery on lower Canyon Road. He hasn't answered his phone all day, so I decided to drive over and see if I could find him. He lives in a small house behind the gallery. But there's a 'Closed Until Further Notice' sign posted on the door of the gallery. I thought you should know."

He told Antonio about what he'd seen at Jimmy's studio last night. "Looks like the two of them might have taken off together."

"What's our next move?"

"Meet me at the station. I'm headed there now. By the way, have you questioned Rose Lucero yet?"

"No, I haven't caught up with her yet."

"Good. Don't bother. I think I better deal with Rose."

8

Fernando parked his car in the Washington Avenue station lot and walked across the Plaza to the Starbucks for a decent cup of coffee. By this time of morning the line of tourists in front of him stretched nearly to the door, so he waited impatiently for over ten minutes for one damn cup of coffee. That was the danger of living in a town overrun with tourists. No service for locals.

He found Antonio already waiting for him in his office. The big man's legs reached halfway across the room, his huge frame barely fitting in the metal chair facing the desk.

Antonio shook his head. "So Jimmy's run?"

"Looks like it. And Blaine might have gone with him."

"You want me to put out an APB?" Antonio asked.

"Yeah, right away. They could already be out of New Mexico."

After Antonio left, he opened the bottom drawer of his desk and put his feet up to think. Now what? He couldn't sit around here waiting for someone to respond to the APB.

Moments later the desk phone rang. "Please hold for the Mayor," a woman's voice said.

He held, expecting the worst. He wasn't disappointed.

"Detective Lopez, is it true you let my wife's killer escape?"

Fernando sputtered. "Well...no...I didn't have anything to do with releasing Jimmy. The District Attorney didn't have enough evidence to file charges so they had to let him go. We don't know who killed your wife."

"But it was his knife. He killed her with one of his steak knives," Martin insisted.

"We can't prove that. There were no fingerprints or DNA on the knife."

Martin sounded angry now. "Get serious. It was Mackey's knife. Find him and put him back in jail."

"And there were several other people at Jimmy's house that night...." he started to say, but Martin had already slammed down the phone.

Martin wanted the case opened and closed, tied up in a neat little ribbon. Wouldn't it be nice if things were that easy? There was one little problem: the burden of proof. They had no hard evidence that Jimmy stabbed Kim Martin. The entire case was circumstantial, which Jimmy's lawyer, the infamous Raoul Garcia, would rip to shreds in front of a jury. He knew that, the Chief knew that, the District Attorney knew that, only a fucking politician like Joe Martin did not.

For lack of a better idea he decided to pay Rose Lucero a visit. Something about the way she reacted to Ruby's comment about Kim sleeping with everyone in the group bothered him. She ran off to the bathroom and didn't return. Why? Was she that embarrassed?

He finished his coffee, now lukewarm, and tossed the cup in the trash. Then he walked up Marcy Street to the office of the *Independent*. He found her sitting at her terminal in the rear of the newsroom. He waved. She looked away.

Not waiting for an invitation Fernando walked through the newsroom and took a seat next to hers. She looked pained to see him. Her prim little mouth shut tight as a clenched fist.

"I was hoping you'd be here," Fernando said.

"Detective Lopez, what can I do for you?"

Fernando couldn't help asking, 'Why are you so nervous?"

She blushed. "Well, a man was murdered. You're searching for the killer. And here you are. Why wouldn't I be nervous?"

"Only if you had something to hide," he shot back.

"No, I have nothing to hide. I think Ruby told you everything–"

"I'd like to hear your version of what happened at El Farol that night," Fernando said, staring at Rose. "Ruby said she and Jimmy were arguing over money. Is that right?"

"Walking to his studio, yes. At El Farol Jimmy was drunk and obnoxious and arguing with everyone, including Ruby. That's why the bartender asked us to leave. Forced us to leave, really."

"All of you were asked to leave?" Fernando asked.

She nodded. "Jimmy was going on and on about how he'd wasted a whole year of his life with Ruby when he should have been sleeping with Kim Martin, because Kim was so much better in bed than Ruby. Except he went into great detail about their bodies and the things they liked to do in bed. Nasty stuff like that. Finally Ruby screamed at him to shut up and threw a glass of wine in his face. Then Jimmy tried to slap her, but Blaine managed to hold him back. In their struggle they knocked over some chairs and spilled a pitcher of beer on the floor. That's when the bartender told us to leave."

Fernando nodded. "Had you seen them getting violent with each other before?"

"Well...I've seen them get into shoving matches before, usually when they're drinking. But this time was different. Both of them were enraged. I thought Jimmy was really going to hurt her."

Fernando didn't like what he was hearing. "What about Blaine? What was he doing while Ruby and Jimmy were arguing?"

"He was talking with Dave and Wayne about his gallery. They accused him of favoring Jimmy and not giving them their own shows, as he did for Jimmy. They were jealous."

"But they never got violent."

"Right. I mean, who would want to get in a fight with Blaine?" Rose asked. "He's huge."

Fernando laughed. "Back to Jimmy. Did he say anything that would indicate he was angry with Kim?"

She blushed. "No, he praised her, saying she was amazing in bed. Nothing angry or insulting."

He pondered for a long moment. "What about you? How well did you know Kim?"

"Not well. I'm new in town. I only moved to Santa Fe six months ago."

"But Ruby said all of you were intimate with Kim, including you," Fernando said. "Well...okay, a couple of times. Along with Ruby."

"A threesome?"

Rose did not respond.

Fernando paused a moment and then asked, "Were you jealous of Kim?"

"No! No way." she said angrily. "Why do you ask that?"

"Because you and Ruby seem what...close?"

"That's none of your business." She stood up from her terminal and pointed to the door. "Our conversation is finished."

Fernando watched Rose walk out of the newsroom and disappear down the back hallway toward the restrooms. Disappearing down back hallways was getting to be a habit with her.

Before leaving he placed a card on her desk. Just in case. You never knew what she might remember. Or choose to remember.

9

Leaving the *Independent*, Fernando debated what to do next. Should he head back to the station or take an early lunch? Better to stay clear of the station, he decided. Just in case the Mayor showed up asking why they hadn't found his wife's killer. So instead he said the hell with it and walked over to the Shed for lunch. He considered texting Antonio for company but changed his mind because he was tired of paying for Antonio's lunches. The big man was a mooch, an expensive mooch, given the amount of food he could put away at one sitting.

He walked across the colorful patio, decorated in bright purple and turquoise with red umbrellas over the tables. Already a crowd of rowdies had gathered at the bar inside, swilling beers and margaritas despite the early hour. There was always a festive atmosphere at the Shed, from the moment they opened to the moment the last drunk stumbled out into the moonlight.

He knew all the servers at the Shed by name. Joanne, one of the older servers, spotted him from across the room and waved. "Your friend is already here," she said. "Follow me to your table."

"What? No...." He tried to stop her.

Too late. He spotted Antonio at the small table by the window where they usually sat.

Antonio waved him over. "I thought you might be here so I took the liberty of getting us a table."

"So I see."

"I had to get out of the station. The Mayor's over there berating the Chief and anyone else who'll listen to him."

Fernando took his usual seat at the table with his back to the front door. "I'm beginning to think Martin is a real prick."

"Yeah, I never liked him," Antonio offered.

Joanne reappeared with two glasses of water. "What will you gentlemen have? The usual."

He nodded, but Antonio looked over the menu as if searching for something new he hadn't ordered before. Good luck with that. The Shed hadn't changed their menu in a decade.

"I'd like the chicken enchiladas with red chile and an order of beef tacos on the side."

Fernando laughed. "Are you sure you don't want to add a combination plate for an appetizer?"

Antonio looked at him with a pained expression on his face. "I'm hungry, okay?"

Joanne wrote down their orders and then asked, "And two mocha cakes for desert, right?"

"And coffee," Antonio said.

He stared at Antonio after Joanne left. He started to say something but caught himself.

"So what's the plan?" Antonio asked. "I'd stay away from the station for a while."

"I thought I might go over to Blaine's gallery," Fernando said. "Take a look around, even if he's not there."

When the food arrived, there was barely enough room for all their plates on the small table. Antonio wolfed down his food as though he hadn't eaten for a week. Maybe he hadn't.

He knew Antonio lived by himself in a primitive cabin at the edge of the national forest near Pecos, about twenty miles east of Santa Fe. The big man had been married years ago, but PTSD and episodes of violence resulting from his service in the First Iraq War had ended his marriage. Since then he'd lived alone, having decided he was temperamentally unfit for marriage. He was a damned fine marine and a damned fine cop, but a lousy husband.

As always, he paid for the meal as soon as they finished their mocha cake. They walked back to the station together. Antonio went inside hoping the Mayor had gone back to city hall, while he took the Plymouth and drove back up to Canyon Road.

Approaching Blaine's gallery he spotted a Molly Maid car parked in the driveway. One of the maids carried cleaning supplies from the car to the front porch, where another maid unlocked the door and held it open.

He parked behind the Molly Maid's white Ford Fiesta. The maids watched him walk to the porch. The two women looked to be in their late twenties or early thirties.

The young woman holding the door held up a key. "We're here to clean the house--we're not breaking in."

He laughed. "I know. I'm just looking for Blaine. He seems to have disappeared."

He showed them his badge and introduced himself.

Relieved, the two women stepped inside the gallery. He followed, interpreting their silence as an invitation to enter. Legally questionable--but who would ever find out?

He followed them into the main gallery, where he saw Jimmy's paintings along one entire wall, the usual landscapes and Chopped Nudes. The other walls displayed a mixture of Indian themed paintings, everything from Zuñi dancers to paintings of world famous Taos Pueblo. The prices of the paintings shocked him. They ranged in price from $2,000 for a relatively small canvas to $25,000 for the larger ones. Back in his day you could buy a house in Santa Fe for $25,000. Times had changed and not for the better.

The maids ignored him, busy setting up their cleaning supplies in the rear office. That allowed him freedom to inspect the various rooms. Off to the side he found a small gallery marked 'Photographs by Blaine Rogers.' He took one step inside and stopped dead in his tracks. He stood looking at four walls covered with dozens of 16x20 photographs of a nude Kim Martin. Some were color, some were black and white, but all of them revealed a sexed-up Kim rolling on the floor or on a mattress holding a variety of objects. He'd almost forgotten how drop-dead beautiful she was--a goddess, as Ruby described her.

He couldn't take his eyes off that luscious body. Special lighting heightened the effect of the photographs, with shadows teasing the viewer by revealing just enough of the erogenous zones to titillate. Not exactly pornographic, but not exactly not pornographic, he thought. But he knew the law. No judge or prosecutor would find the photos lacked artistic merit and therefore met the legal standard for obscenity. It was nearly impossible to get an obscenity conviction these days. Every damned pornographer claimed artistic merit.

He moved on to the next small room, which proved to be the studio where presumably Blaine shot his photos of Kim. A large box camera attached to a tripod overlooked a mattress on the floor, with a black cloth hanging on the wall for a backdrop. He shook his head. Blaine would only have to put a video camera on the tripod and he could shoot porno films here. Maybe he did. It seemed anyone could be a pornographer in the age of online porn.

So Kim was not only Blaine's muse, she was his artistic subject. He didn't know what to make of that.

When the maids finished cleaning the office, he helped himself to a look around. No doubt the 27-inch iMac on Blaine's desk contained the gallery's financial and inventory records. He found the desk drawers unlocked and overflowing with old receipts and invoices and brochures of one kind or another. Nothing caught his attention except for a series of brochures from Ghost Ranch. Why so many?

The brochures described the various workshops and programs sponsored by the nonprofit ranch, located about sixty miles north of Santa Fe on U.S. Highway 84. Among them he found brochures on men's and women's wellness programs as well as creative writing and photography workshops. His eyes lit up when he saw that Blaine Rogers was scheduled to teach a workshop on photographing the human body beginning next Monday morning. That was four days away.

Smiling, he tucked one of the photo workshop brochures in his rear pocket for safekeeping.

On the way out he stepped quietly past the studio where the maids were cleaning now, hoping to escape without being noticed. Maybe they would forget they'd seen him. No memory, no foul.

10

They were sitting in his office comparing notes. Fernando had his feet up on his desk with his notebook cradled in his lap. Antonio sat backwards on the metal chair with his arms folded over the back of the chair facing him. They went down the list of the five people whose paths had crossed at Jimmy's studio the night Kim was murdered. By agreement they omitted peripheral characters like Dave and Wayne at El Farol and the Bryans, Paul and June, from Essentia next door.

They started with Jimmy.

"He had the opportunity, but what about motive?" Antonio asked.

"He was crazy drunk and didn't know what he was doing," Fernando said. "How's that?"

Antonio nodded. "Ruby?"

"Ruby said she left before Kim arrived, but I wonder," Fernando said. "For motive, how about Jealousy? Say what you will about their marriage being over, she was jealous of Kim for fucking Jimmy."

"And Rose?"

"Same as Ruby," Fernando said. "She was jealous of Kim for fucking Ruby, one of her lovers."

Antonio nodded. "And she had the same story about leaving early. Conveniently."

"Which brings us to Blaine," Fernando said. "He stayed on with Jimmy arguing about business the night Kim was murdered, and it looks as though he was the person who attacked Jimmy last night. Not to mention he has a reputation for violent behavior."

"But what's his motive?" Antonio asked.

"Good question. He's the wild card, the mystery man."

"Yeah, because why would Blaine kill Kim, the model he used in his photos and the source of at least some of his income?" Antonio asked.

Fernando pondered Antonio's question. "I don't know. Something's missing. We're not there yet."

"I guess we can rule out suicide."

"Yeah, why would she kill herself now, just as she was about to get rid of her husband and receive a hefty settlement?" Fernando asked. "Plus she was a sex goddess. She was sleeping with everyone in the group and apparently enjoying it."

"Mm-hmm."

"But let's don't omit the obvious," Fernando said.

Antonio smiled. "Of course, the angry husband. He claims to have an alibi for that night, but no corroboration. And he certainly had the motive."

"True...but I don't know," Fernando said. "I just can't see Joe Martin sticking a steak knife in his wife's chest. He just doesn't seem like the kind of man who would let his passions get the better of him. He's too cold blooded."

"Yeah, like a goddamned fish," Antonio said.

They sat in silence for several minutes. Fernando continued to scribble in his notebook waiting for an epiphany, a moment of insight. None came.

A few minutes later his desk phone rang. He answered and heard the familiar voice of Linda from the front counter.

"Fernando, we just got a response to our APB. A clerk at a Walgreen's up in Española reported seeing the two guys described in the bulletin and the green L.L. Bean Subaru Outback. He said they stopped at the liquor department and bought several bottles of hard liquor and a case of beer and took off like a bat out of hell driving North on Highway 84. He described the two as agitated and belligerent. Does that sound about right?"

"Yeah, I'd say that was a pretty good description of the two of them. What's the clerk's name?" he asked, reaching for his pen.

"Steven Montoya. He didn't know where the two men were headed, just that they were driving north."

He recorded the information in his notebook and then tossed it on the desk. "No matter. I think I know where they're going."

Antonio stared at him. "What did you say?"

He took the Ghost Ranch brochure out of his back pocket and handed it to Antonio. "Take a look."

Antonio's eyes skimmed over the brochure. "Hah! Blaine's teaching a photography workshop. Starting on Monday. That's four days from now. So what's your plan?"

"Let's leave first thing tomorrow morning," Fernando said. "It'll take us at least an hour and a half to get up there. We'll surprise them and maybe get a better sense of what the hell happened at Jimmy's studio. I'll ask the Chief if he wants us to arrest Jimmy and bring him in again."

They agreed to meet at the station tomorrow morning at eight sharp.

After Antonio left, he closed his office door for privacy and tried to dredge up his memory of Ghost Ranch. He'd spent a week there many years ago when the Santa Fe Police Department sponsored a summer camp for disadvantaged kids. He remembered the office and a scattering of ramshackle buildings, mostly cabins and bunkhouses and mess halls for the guests. There was also a campground and a series of corrals for the ranch's horses.

Lots of folks around Northern New Mexico considered Ghost Ranch a haunted place. If he remembered correctly the rumors began in the 1880s when the owners, the Archuleta Brothers, named the property *Rancho de los Brujos*. The brothers, notorious cattle rustlers, stole cattle and horses and hid them in the box canyon behind the ranch. They chose the name Ranch of the Witches to scare away farmers and ranchers who came looking for their stolen livestock. Rumor had it the brothers murdered those who continued to search for their animals and buried the bodies in the canyon or tossed them into wells. Ghost stories soon followed. Locals claimed to hear the voices of murder victims in the howling winds blowing through the canyon. Some saw strange lights moving through the buildings, especially around "Ghost House," where the brothers had lived.

Predictably, the Archuleta Brothers met a grisly fate. One brother killed the other during an argument over booty. The surviving brother died soon after, hung by an angry posse for a life of cattle rustling and murder. Their voices joined the chorus of the other ghosts.

Today locals and guests still claimed to hear a myriad of voices wailing in the canyon. He remembered sleeping uneasily in the dilapidated wooden bunkhouse during the week he'd spent there at summer camp.

At night some of the kids claimed to hear screams. Others claimed to see objects moving in the darkness. The experience rattled his nerves. By week's end, suffering from insomnia, he'd vowed to never again step foot on *Ranchos de los Brujos*.

But now, it seemed, he had no choice.

11

They passed through Abiquiu, the mesa-top village made famous by Georgia O'Keeffe, and arrived at Ghost Ranch by mid morning. Fernando turned right onto the primitive road leading into the sprawling property surrounded by distant mesas and jagged cliffs. The road curved around toward the massive Kitchen Mesa, with a maze of roads connecting the various buildings off to the left. He steered into the parking lot in front of the Welcome Center and watched Antonio jump out of their cruiser mumbling to himself.

"What a dump," Antonio said, stretching his back. At six feet, seven inches tall the big man suffered when confined in a small space for any length of time.

He had to agree with Antonio. "Doesn't look like it's changed much in twenty years."

Fernando surveyed the ramshackle wooden building with wings and add-ons jutting out in myriad directions. On the long porch a couple of old timers wearing western hats sat on a bench jawing.

He led the way, walking up the steps and into a dark hallway, his heavy walking shoes echoing on the plank floor. The rough-cut wood and western décor made you feel like you were walking back in time a hundred years.

"Howdy," a man behind the counter greeted them, coming forward into the light.

Antonio jumped back, surprised by the man's voice.

Fernando turned around to find a grizzled, bewhiskered man wearing a baseball cap and a kerchief around his neck. "Didn't see you back there."

The man smiled.

Fernando showed his badge and identified himself. "We're looking for two men who we think arrived yesterday, Blaine Rogers and Jimmy Mackey. Rogers is scheduled to teach a photography workshop on Monday."

The man's smile faded. "Those two. Yeah, they checked in yesterday afternoon and caused quite a ruckus. You here to arrest them?"

"Not at the moment," Fernando said. "What kind of ruckus did they cause?"

'Well, we put them in one of our casitas over near the Arts Center. Casita Number Three. 'Bout five o'clock we started getting calls from other guests saying the two were raising hell, fighting and busting up the casita. When we got there, both Rogers and Mackey were drunk as all get out and crazy as hell. We would have thrown them out if the big one didn't have a workshop on Monday. The little one was getting the worst of it, so we took him out and put him up in the Pine Cottage nearby where we could keep an eye on him. He took quite a lickin'."

"Where's the Pine Cottage?"

"Here," the man said, handing him a map of Ghost Ranch. "Right behind Ghost House, a couple of doors down the lane."

The man behind the desk glanced at Antonio. "That Rogers fella is about your size."

"Not even close," Antonio shot back. "I got three inches and forty pounds on him. If he gives you any more trouble, just let us know."

"Have you seen them today yet?" Fernando asked.

"Haven't seen hide nor hair of either one," the man said. "If you do see them, tell 'em to lay off the booze. They're a coupla mean drunks."

"Yes they are."

They walked back out to the car to conference.

"Which one of the mean drunks do you wanna visit first?" Antonio asked.

"Let's start with Blaine and then come back around to the Pine Cottage." He checked the map of Ghost Ranch they'd been given and found Casita Number Three on the map.

They followed the main road east around the Arts Center to a large parking lot near a bathhouse. The casitas perched on top of a hill overlooking the bathhouse, seven of them built in a neat row.

They climbed up a narrow dirt path to the casitas, tiny houses with poured concrete slabs for porches, each with a chair outside the door.

Fernando stepped up to the door of number three and pounded. When no one answered he pounded again, louder.

"What? Leave me alone."

Fernando pounded again. "Open up, Blaine. This is Detective Lopez from the Santa Fe Police Department."

"Go away. I said leave me alone, can't you fucking hear?"

With that, the door burst open and Blaine stepped outside on the porch bumping into Fernando, not accidentally. "What the hell do you want?" he asked in a slightly calmer voice, a big man with a potbelly wearing Bermuda shorts and a Zozobra T-shirt. His raven black hair was long and disheveled and hung down across his forehead. He had a scratch above his left eyebrow and a black eye. Not a pretty sight for someone preparing to teach a photography workshop.

Fernando showed his badge and introduced himself and Antonio properly. "We need to ask you some questions about the night Kim Martin was murdered at Jimmy Mackey's studio. Do you mind?" He brushed past Blaine, not waiting for an answer.

Antonio followed, shoving Blaine out of the way.

Blaine glared at Antonio, not used to being pushed around. Few people in Santa Fe were as large or as intimidating as Antonio. If any.

"Kim was a friend of yours," Fernando said, trying a different tact. "Help us find her murderer and bring him to justice. It's the least we can do for her."

That seemed to placate Blaine, who rubbed his forehead and pushed the hair back out of his eyes. "Yeah...I guess."

Blaine sat down on a sagging chair while they looked around the tiny casita, no more than a sitting room with twin cots in the rear. One step up from camping.

They sat down on a beat-up loveseat facing the chair, ignoring the broken glass on the floor and a busted wooden nightstand in the corner.

"So, Blaine, what happened between you and Jimmy? Why'd they have to move him to another unit?" Fernando asked.

"Hah! Goddamn Jimmy. We had a few drinks and then he started in on me. He's always bugging me to give him another show, always another show, he's never satisfied. I keep telling him his shit doesn't sell like it used to, but he doesn't believe me. The tourists are more sophisticated these days, they don't want the same old tired landscapes, and that's all Jimmy can do anymore. Except for his Chopped Nude series, which is good but not something the tourists want. Man, I had a couple from Texas come in the other day and they took one look at a Chopped Nude and ran out of the gallery saying it was Satanic. Motherfucking satanic. I kid you not. That's a true story. So, yeah, I told Jimmy to fuck off, I'm not giving him another show until he paints something I can fucking sell."

Fernando couldn't help but laugh. "So you started fighting?"

"Yeah, we broke the table and a bottle or two, nothing serious. I didn't hurt him, if that's what you mean. Hell, we'll meet for breakfast tomorrow and make up, like we always do."

"And you guys do this frequently, right? In fact, you were fighting last night at Jimmy's studio."

"Yeah, because he's always broke. He's always asking for money. This time I said NO, I wouldn't give him another fucking penny unless he came along and helped me set up my photography workshop here and helped me out whenever I needed it. Which is why he's here now."

Fernando nodded. "Okay, back to the night Kim was murdered. You were at Jimmy's studio that night. In fact, you were the last to leave before Kim arrived. Or were you still there when she came?"

"No, after Ruby and Rose left I stayed for a few minutes talking business with Jimmy and then walked down to my gallery. About halfway there I saw Kim driving up Canyon Road. Funny, though, she wasn't alone. There was someone with her in the car."

"A second person?"

"Yep. I didn't get a good look, but someone was sitting in the passenger's seat," Blaine said.

Fernando and Antonio looked at each other.

"Do you have any idea who would want to harm Kim?" Fernando asked. "Enemies, former lovers, whatever?"

"Well, usually in these cases it's the husband, right," Blaine said. "Joe Martin is a jealous prick, a fucking asshole. Kim was sleeping around because he couldn't perform, so why wouldn't he be pissed?"

"But all of you in that group were sleeping with Kim, according to Ruby," Fernando said. "You were romantically involved with her too, right?"

Blaine laughed. "Romantically involved? You sound like you're in high school."

Fernando shrugged. "Maybe you were jealous."

"Nah, I don't take it that seriously. It's just getting laid, man. No big deal. Although I'll have to admit, Kim was as good as they get. She had moves I can't even describe."

“So everyone says. Except her husband.”

Blaine laughed. “Fucking Joe Martin. What an ass.”

Fernando stood up and nodded to Antonio. “Well...I understand you’ll be teaching a photography workshop here next week.”

“Yeah, it starts on Monday. I’ll be here all week.”

“Will Jimmy be staying all week too?” Fernando asked.

Blaine shrugged. “I don’t know. He’s supposed to help me out with the class, but half the time he doesn’t even show up. He gets distracted, you know. Loses interest. Then he just wonders off like a crazy man. Disappears. I think he’s mental.”

“Okay then. We know where to find you,” Fernando said, motioning for Antonio to follow.

They walked outside into the late afternoon light that lit up Kitchen Mesa behind them and Pedernal Butte to the south. The entire canyon was bathed in the rich golden glow of autumn.

“Quite a pair,” Antonio mumbled as they walked down the dirt path to their car.

12

They followed the main road back toward the Welcome Center and turned right at Ghost House, where the infamous Archuleta Brothers had lived back in the late 1800s. The rugged structure fit the bill, shrouded by a curving adobe wall and protected by bleached steer skulls attached to the front of the house. Their empty eyes watched them turn the corner and proceed up the short drive. Rumor had it that the ghosts of the two brothers still inhabited Ghost House, while the ghosts of all those they had murdered roamed by night over the entire ranch. Legions of ghosts.

Fernando saw Jimmy's green Subaru as they approached Pine Cottage, about the size of Ghost House. He pulled in behind the Subaru and set the brake. Antonio waited by the car while he walked up to the door and knocked. When no one answered he knocked again but with the same result. He tried the door and found it unlocked, so he invited himself in and looked around. No sign of Jimmy, but he saw a backpack stuffed with clothing tossed on a worn sofa in the sitting room. The cottage looked larger than Blaine's casita, with a more spacious sitting area, twin double beds, and a bath with a shower.

On a side table next to the sofa were two bottles of vodka, one full and the other two-thirds empty. Jimmy didn't travel far without his bottle.

He heard Antonio come in behind him, his boots clomping on the wooden floor.

"This place looks a little better," Antonio said.

"Some. There's a toilet over there if you need it."

They helped themselves to the facilities and then went outside to sit on the bench in front of the cottage waiting for Jimmy to reappear.

It didn't take long for waiting to get boring, so they took turns walking around Ghost Ranch in and out of the *cul de sacs* and the narrow lanes lined with ramshackle buildings. The place wasn't much to look at, but it had that feeling of being inhabited by a presence, something ancient. That presence, whatever it was, seemed very close to the surface of consciousness. He couldn't describe the feeling any better than that. He didn't like to admit--to himself or anyone else-- that he believed in ghosts. Still, he knew what he'd seen at Chaco Canyon this past summer right before his accident. If that wasn't a ghost, then what the hell was it?

Toward evening Jimmy hadn't reappeared, so they sat on the bench outside to discuss what to do next. Finally Fernando said, "We'll have to spend the night. What else can we do?"

Antonio nodded. "Suit yourself. You're the one with a wife at home. I don't care either way."

So Fernando left Antonio at the Pine Cottage and walked to the Welcome Center. The grizzled cowboy at the front desk greeted him when he stepped inside. "Welcome, friend. Did you fellers find those two guys?"

"We found Blaine Rogers, but Jimmy's not at the Pine Cottage. Is there an event going on here tonight that might explain why he's not at the cottage?"

"Nope. Not a thing. You say he hasn't been back?"

"Right. We've been there all day waiting for him.

"Hmmm...imagine that."

Fernando shrugged. "So I guess we'll spend the night. Can you give us another cottage close to Pine?"

The cowboy looked at his booking sheet. "Sure can. I can give you Juniper next door."

"Okay. Let's do it." He filled out the reservation form and paid with a credit card.

The cowboy gave him the key and pointed out Juniper Cottage on his map. "It's right here, the second cottage up from Ghost House."

"Tell me about Ghost House? Should we be worried?" Fernando asked, half joking.

"Hah! Only if you go there after dark."

"Yeah?"

The cowboy looked around the office and then turned back to him. "Ho boy, I could tell you some stories. Thing is, we're not supposed to talk about the ghosts or whatever they are. Management won't let us. They say it scares away the guests. Me, I don't know about that. I think maybe people would come just to see the ghosts. Maybe go ghost hunting. What do you think?"

"Not sure," Fernando said. "I can see both sides of the argument. Might scare away the tourists, but the local loonies would probably love it."

The man smiled. "I like that, local loonies. Ain't it the truth?"

Outside the Welcome Center Fernando sat on a bench and called Estelle to tell her he wouldn't be home until tomorrow. Then he walked over to the Cantina and bought a sandwich and a bottle of water for himself, and two sandwiches and two bottles of water for Antonio. By the time he made it back to the Pine Cottage Antonio was pacing out front.

"Good, you brought some food. I'm starving."

"Yeah, but wait a minute," Fernando said. "I rented the cottage next door. Let's move the cruiser around back. That way Jimmy won't know we're waiting for him."

Fernando drove the car up behind the Juniper Cottage and parked it out of sight. Antonio carried the food and drinks to the porch while Fernando opened the door. When he flipped the light switch he heard the scampering of little feet on the wooden floor. Rodents.

Antonio cursed. "Jesus, you gotta wonder how long this place has been vacant. Smells like the inside of an abandoned house full of something nasty."

"Thanks. I just lost my appetite."

"Not me. I can eat," Antonio said. He pulled a couple of chairs over to a small table in the sitting room and waited.

Fernando took the sandwiches and bottles of water out of the bag and placed them on the table. Antonio didn't waste any time, devouring his first sandwich by the time he'd removed his one sandwich from the plastic wrapper.

After they finished Antonio looked around for the automatic coffee maker? "What, no coffee?"

'This isn't the Holiday Inn."

"That's for sure. The Holiday Inn doesn't have rats."

"What we heard are probably just mice. Don't worry. They don't have as much Plague or Hanta Virus."

Antonio glanced at him. "If I catch the Plague, I'll fucking kill Jimmy."

They spent the evening listening to rodents scurrying under the floorboards and behind the baseboards and discussing ways to torture

Jimmy when they finally caught up with the sonofabitch.

Eventually they gave up and got settled for the night. They dusted off the pillows and blankets on the beds, deciding to watch for Jimmy in shifts. Fernando took the first shift because he couldn't bear the thought of sleeping in the dusty, uninviting bed until he was dead tired. Instead, he set up a chair by a side window that overlooked Pine Cottage, while Antonio slept.

He sat back in the chair and tried to stay awake, his eyelids growing heavy.

13

Fernando's head snapped forward when he heard the noise. He checked his watch: nearly Midnight. The sound of humming seemed to come from down the lane near Ghost House. He stumbled out of his chair, sending the chair careening across the room. Outside in the darkness he saw lights moving slowly up the lane toward them. Still groggy, he staggered to the door and flung it open, waking Antonio who had been snoring on the bed.

"What is it?" Antonio asked, reaching for his boots.

"Ghosts."

Fernando stepped outside and looked around. The cold night air hit him like a slap across the face. Up ahead he saw the light moving closer, bobbing and weaving as it approached. He watched as the shape of a human materialized out of the darkness. The mysterious figure pulled a large bag behind him, toboggan style. Something howled out in the darkness, possibly the wind.

Antonio came up behind him growling and cursing, not a happy camper. "What time is it, for fuck's sake?"

"Midnight."

Approaching them, the apparition continued humming an old Beatles' tune: "Oh I get by with a little help from me friends...mmm I get high with a little help from me friends."

Fernando realized the bouncing light came from a headband worn by the apparition, who he now recognized.

"It's Jimmy," he whispered to Antonio.

Jimmy stopped when he saw them standing next to his Subaru. He looked around. “Oh, fuck. Not you, Lopez. You’re the kind of person who rains on every parade. A downer.”

“Nice to see you too, Jimmy. At first I thought you were a ghost.”

“Nah, they’re back at Ghost House and over by the corral. I saw two of them on my way back here, big fuckers. Just walk away. They won’t hurt you.”

Antonio continued to curse.

“So what do you want now?” Jimmy asked.

“I need to ask you some questions about the night Kim was murdered. You were told to stay in Santa Fe. Why’d you run?”

“Run? Come on, man. I didn’t run. I’m here working with Blaine, the greedy motherfucker. I already told the cops everything I remember about that night. I was drunk and passed out. I don’t know who killed her.”

While he talked, Jimmy opened the back hatch of his Subaru and tossed in the duffel bag, which landed with a loud clank next to some camping gear.

“Do you remember Kim arriving that night?”

Jimmy shook his head. “No, the last thing I remember is fighting with Blaine. He won’t give me another show until I give the tourists what they want. Shit! That’s what they want. Hah!”

“So you didn’t see Kim at all that night? Is that what you’re saying.”

“Right. I didn’t see her until the cops opened the trunk of her car.” Jimmy pointed to Antonio. “Frankenstein was there. He should remember that.”

Antonio gritted his teeth.

“But Kim was killed by one of your steak knives. How do you explain that?” Fernando asked.

“Someone must have come into my studio and taken one of the knives. Geez. Gimme a break.”

“Like who? Who was there when Kim arrived?”

“Fuck if I know. I told you. I was drunk.”

“I think you’re lying,” Fernando said.

“Yeah, well you guys can stay out here all night for all I care, but I need a drink,” Jimmy said and walked past them into Pine Cottage.

While Jimmy headed inside, Fernando moved to the rear of the Subaru and took a look at Jimmy’s duffel bag. In the bag he found a hammer and crowbar and a selection of other tools, including saws.

Fernando put the tools back in the duffel bag, closed the back of the

Subaru, and followed the others into the cottage. Once inside he watched Jimmy make a bee-line for the full bottle of vodka on the table beside the sofa. Jimmy found a plastic glass in the bathroom and filled it with vodka, downing the first glass in a matter of seconds and then refilling the glass to the brim.

Jimmy shivered. "Oh yeah."

"So Jimmy, before you pass out and don't remember anything, tell me this. What the hell are you doing walking around at night with a bag of tools?"

"Yeah...see...Blaine has this gig starting Monday," Jimmy said. "He's teaching a photo workshop and the classroom needs some work. Everything here's old, man. This place gives me the creeps, especially with the ghosts everywhere."

"Don't start," Antonio said.

"Didn't you see the one following me up from Ghost House? I don't know what he wanted, but he followed me all the way back here. You can tell when they're near. There's a coldness in the air, a chill."

The three of them sat on the lumpy chairs in the sitting room listening to Jimmy's ghost stories for several long minutes. By then Jimmy had finished nearly half of the bottle of vodka.

Fernando stood up finally and said, "Time to get some sleep. We need to get you back to Santa Fe early tomorrow."

"Oh, man. Blaine's gonna be pissed. He wants me to help him with the workshop."

"Not my problem," Fernando said.

Antonio took out his cuffs and headed over to the metal bedframe where Jimmy would sleep.

"Awww, come on, man! Don't cuff me. I've been drinking. I'll have to get up in the middle of the night to pee."

Antonio looked dubious.

"Please. I'm not going anywhere."

"Okay, but don't do anything stupid," Fernando said. "Be ready for breakfast at eight. We'll go to the Dining Hall for breakfast and then leave for Santa Fe. Understand?"

Jimmy smiled. "Have I ever disappointed you, Lopez?"

"Yeah, as a matter of fact. Every time I see you."

Jimmy opened his arms. "I'm a man of peace, just feeling groovy."

14

"Wake up!"

Fernando fought to open his eyes. Antonio was standing over him shaking him by his shoulders. "Jimmy's gone. I knew we should have cuffed him. Goddamnit."

Struggling out of bed, Fernando hobbled over to the side window and looked out. Sure enough, Jimmy's Subaru was gone. He'd absconded during the night.

"Shit," was all he could think to say. Antonio had been right. He should have cuffed Jimmy to the metal bedframe.

Antonio cursed. "I don't know about you, but I'm getting tired of chasing that crazy bastard."

Fernando straitened up and stretched his back muscles. Every muscle in his body ached from sleeping on the sagging mattress. Time to make a plan.

He put on his socks and shoes and went into the bathroom to splash water on his face. He tried to avoid the mirror, but when he caught a glimpse of himself he frowned and turned away. The dark circles under his eyes complemented the deep wrinkles in his forehead. He smoothed back his short salt and pepper hair and dried off with a towel. A man his age should never look into a mirror. That was a fact.

Finished, he looked across the room at Antonio, who was still pissed that Jimmy had escaped.

"Okay. I'll go over to the Cantina for coffee and pastries, whatever you want, and then we'll head back to Santa Fe," Fernando said. "I don't think it'll be hard to find Jimmy. He'll go back to his studio."

"Sounds like a plan. Except instead of coffee and pastries, let's go to the Dining Hall for a full breakfast. I'm starving."

Fernando laughed. "I should have known."

So after Antonio had a chance to clean up, they went to the Dining Hall for a big breakfast, after which they packed up and headed out.

He drove down to the main road leading to the highway. They'd gone a little more than a block when Antonio pointed to the Welcome Center and said, "Look, something's happened. Maybe it's Jimmy."

A Rio Arriba County sheriff's car was parked in front of the Welcome Center and a crowd had gathered on the wooden porch.

Fernando pulled up alongside the other police car and followed Antonio onto the porch. The crowd made way for them when they showed their badges. Inside they found two state police officers talking to the cowboy behind the counter and two maintenance workers from the ranch.

The cop in charge, whose nametag read Taggart, asked the workers, "And you're sure this happened last night?"

"Positive," the older of the two workers said, a wiry little man in overalls. "We were there all day yesterday and saw no evidence of vandalism."

Taggart nodded, a stocky man with a moustache and a deeply tanned face.

He sidled up to Taggart and showed his badge. "What's happened?"

"Someone broke into Casa del Sol, the old adobe that Georgia O'Keeffe used to own back in the thirties. These boys showed up to repair some stucco this morning and found the damage. Sounds like the vandals ripped out a bunch of drywall and some kitchen cabinets. Don't know yet if they were looking to steal copper pipe or what they were looking for."

Taggart turned to the workers. "You want to show us the damage?"

"Sure, just follow our truck."

The crowd of onlookers parted to make way for the entourage. The workers walked outside to their pickup, while Fernando and Antonio and the two state cops climbed into their cruisers.

The pickup led the way down the main road to a dog-leg to the right blocked by a gate. The older worker jumped out of the pickup and unlocked the gate and then proceeded. About a mile down the road they approached a U-shaped adobe with an open courtyard that looked out on Pedernal, the majestic butte that O'Keeffe made famous in so many of her paintings. Her old adobe was surrounded on three sides by rocky mesas that receded into the distance.

They parked along a rattlesnake fence and followed the others to the front door, where the lock had been broken and the door pried open with a crowbar or something heavy. Inside the rooms were painted white and sparsely but tastefully appointed in the best Southwestern style, with paintings, ceramics, and Navajo rugs. Everything looked expensive, which begged the question: why hadn't the intruders taken any of the valuable art works?

The workers took them to a bedroom in a far corner of the house where a closet had been built out from the wall. Inside the closet all the drywall had been ripped out revealing the adobe bricks underneath. Torn and busted pieces of drywall had been tossed haphazardly on the wooden plank floor.

Taggart and the other state cop looked around but said nothing.

Fernando shook his head. "Hard to believe someone would break into a house in the middle of nowhere just to bust up a closet...and without taking any of the art work here."

"Doesn't make sense," Taggart agreed.

"Take a look at the kitchen," one of the workers said. Everyone followed him back to the kitchen in the front of the house. The worker pointed to a grouping of kitchen cabinets that had been pried loose from the wall. One of the cabinets had been ripped completely out of the wall and tossed on the floor. It lay in a pile of busted wood and broken glass.

Taggart inspected the damaged wall and then went through all the cabinets, including the one on the floor. "Couldn't have been looking for drugs. No reason to believe there would be drugs here."

Taggart scratched his head. "And you say these cabinets and the closet were the only places vandalized?"

"As far as we know. And nothing was taken."

While they talked, Fernando and Antonio stepped outside into the courtyard to look around. The view of Pedernal was spectacular. "Not a bad place for an artist like O'Keeffe," Fernando said.

Antonio agreed. "Especially if you like solitude. Like I do."

They walked around the courtyard and the parking area along the fence but found nothing of interest.

Finally they gave up the search and returned to the cruiser. Fernando made a U-turn on the dusty mesa and drove back to the main road, where they turned left and headed back to Santa Fe.

As soon as they were safely on the highway the two of them turned to each other and at the same time said: "Jimmy."

"But why? What the hell was he doing busting up drywall at Casa del Sol?" Fernando asked.

Antonio shook his head. "Fucking artists, they're all crazy."

15

In Santa Fe they stopped first at Jimmy's studio. Fernando walked to the front door while Antonio went around back to check the garage for Jimmy's car. Once on the porch he banged on the door and then stood back. No one answered, so he took out his pick and opened the door himself. Inside the place looked much the same as before, except he found the bedroom closet open and coat hangers scattered on the bed and floor. So Jimmy had been here recently. He must have quickly grabbed a handful of clothes from the closet and stuffed them into a suitcase or backpack and then taken off again.

On his way out he noticed that art supplies on one of the worktables in the studio had been removed. That meant Jimmy had taken some of his art materials with him, wherever he intended to hide out. Everything else looked the same, so he locked up and walked back to their car where Antonio waited impatiently.

The big man shook his head. "His garage is empty."

They leaned against the car discussing what to do next. While they talked, Paul Bryan appeared in the front yard of Essentia and began trimming his hollyhocks. He spotted them and meandered over to talk. "Any news?"

He shook his head. "No, we're still looking for Jimmy. Have you seen him?"

"Yeah, he came by earlier this morning," Paul said, a small man wearing khaki shorts and a black T-shirt with hair moussed to the consistency of gelatin. "He packed some clothes in a backpack and took off again."

"Did he say where?"

"No, he didn't stick around to talk. He seemed in a big hurry. He waved from his porch and then took off in his old Subaru."

"Okay," Fernando said. "Call me right away if he comes back. I gave my card to June yesterday."

"Sure," Paul said, walking away.

Fernando looked at Antonio. "I'm not looking forward to facing the Chief. Let's find Ruby. If anyone knows where Jimmy is, it'll be Ruby."

"Good plan."

They climbed back into the squad car and drove down Canyon Road past El Farol and Blaine's closed gallery. Once on the Paseo they followed it around to the Railyard District.

They parked in front of Ruby's pottery co-op and walked inside. They found one woman with a kerchief tied around her head kneading a hunk of moist brown clay. She wiped her hands on a towel and said, "Yes?"

"We're looking for Ruby," Fernando said.

"She's next door at Emilio's having lunch."

He thanked the woman and followed Antonio outside and into Emilio's Café. They saw Ruby sitting at a booth along the wall eating a salad. Across from her sat Rose Lucero, writing in a small notebook.

Ruby laughed when she saw them. "Well, well, I sure am popular with the police these days. I guess I better call my lawyer. What do you pigs want?"

"We can't stay away, Ruby. You're that enticing," Fernando countered.

Fernando glanced at Rose, who put away her notebook and said, "I'm writing a story about Ruby's pottery co-op."

Fernando squeezed into the booth next to Ruby. Antonio sat next to Rose, who looked embarrassed and very uncomfortable.

Emilio himself came over to the table as soon as they sat down. He was a fat man with a dirty apron tied around his waist and a big smile on his face. "What can I get for you fellers?"

Fernando asked for a bowl of posole. Antonio ordered his usual combination plate.

"So what is it this time?" Ruby asked, putting down her fork and wiping her lips with a napkin.

"Where's Jimmy?" Fernando asked.

"How would I know?"

"Come on, Ruby. You and Jimmy know everything about each other. You might as well still be married. Tell me this, for a man who claims to be innocent, why is he always running away?"

She laughed. "I suppose because you're trying to pin Kim's murder on him, what do you think."

"Why wouldn't I think he's guilty? He keeps running away. Innocent people don't run away."

She shrugged. "Maybe."

"Why do you put up with him anyway?" Fernando asked. "What's the attraction? He's a damn lunatic."

"Yeah, but he's also a charmer...he's endearing. He's the kind of guy every woman wants to take care of. You should try it sometime instead of the macho bullshit."

Fernando turned to look at her squarely in the eyes. "If he's so wonderful, then why did you sleep with his brother and end the marriage? Did you really do that? Sleep with his brother?"

Ruby flipped her wrist. "Just once. So what? That's nothing compared to all Jimmy's transgressions. He was screwing every woman on Canyon Road."

"I can believe that."

She returned to her salad.

"Give me the truth. Where is he?" Fernando asked.

"Do you really want the truth--or do you want some bullshit story you can tell the Chief and then forget about the whole thing?"

"The truth."

"Okay, then," she said. "Jimmy stopped by this morning and hit me up for money. He already owes me a couple of K but I gave him what I had. He said he was leaving town--maybe going down to Jaurez for a while."

Fernando's spirits sank. Just what he needed. A trip to Jaurez, the drug and murder capitol of the Western Hemisphere.

When Emilio brought their food, he pushed aside his bowl of posole. Antonio began wolfing down his combination plate.

Rose, who wasn't eating, watched Antonio eat with a horrified look on her face.

"We were just up at Ghost Ranch chasing Jimmy," Fernando said. "He was staying with Blaine until the two of them got into some kind of fight yesterday. Then last night someone broke into the O'Keeffe house up there. Casa del Sol. We think it might be Jimmy because we saw a bag of tools in his car. He took off again this morning, so we're still chasing him."

"Oh, Jesus, it's that crazy fucking Blaine," Ruby said. "He controls Jimmy like a puppet because his gallery is where Jimmy sells all his work. Whatever Blaine wants, Jimmy does. No questions asked."

Fernando frowned. "What about Casa del Sol? Why would Blaine want Jimmy to break into the O'Keeffe house?"

Ruby sighed. "Because of a rumor. Wayne, one of the old drunks at El Farol, says his father worked for O'Keeffe as a handyman at Casa del Sol. Wayne says his father told him O'Keeffe hid a painting in the walls of the house that she didn't want anyone to see during her lifetime. Some end-of-the-world painting of a blood red sky over a mesa composed of human bones. I'm sure it's all bullshit."

Fernando nodded. "And Jimmy does pretty much anything Blaine wants him to do?"

"Like I said, he's Blaine's puppet."

Fernando retrieved his cast-off bowl of posole and then had second thoughts and pushed it away again. "Here's another question for the two of you. You both said you left Jimmy's studio early the night Kim was murdered. Blaine left after you. He told us he saw Kim driving up Canyon Road as he walked down to his gallery. He said he saw two people in Kim's car. That second person could have been the murderer. Did either of you see Kim's car when you left?"

Ruby shook her head.

"Actually, I did," Rose said. "I walked down Canyon Road back to my apartment on Don Gaspar. Just as I came to the Paseo I saw Kim turn onto Canyon Road. But she was alone. There was no one else in the car."

Ruby finished her salad and elbowed him in the ribs to let her out. She climbed out of the booth and said, "Well boys and girls, this has been a real love fest, but I have a business to run." She threw a ten spot on the table and walked out.

Rose seemed embarrassed to be alone with them. "I guess I should go too...."

Antonio stood up to let her out. She hurried out of the café without looking back.

Fernando left a twenty on the table and followed Antonio outside. The big man stopped him on the porch. "Count me out for Juarez. That's a death sentence."

Fernando ignored the comment.

Just as they reached the car his cell phone rang.

"Fernando, the Chief wants to see you right away," Linda said. "Forensics found Kim's blood on one of Jimmy's shirts. An arrest warrant has been issued."

"No kidding."

"They found the shirt at the bottom of a laundry bag in his closet. The stains were small, but enough to get a match. Chief's waiting for you now."

He turned to Antonio. "We have the evidence we need. Forensics found Kim's blood on Jimmy's shirt."

16

Chief Stuart stood at his office window looking out on Washington Avenue. He shook his head. "Juarez? Damn! That could be a problem. We have an extradition treaty with Mexico, but with the cartels and the border issues...it could take years to get him out of Juarez. No, the best thing to do would be to give him the option to come back peacefully. Otherwise he faces months in a Mexican jail. Nobody wants to spend months in a Mexican jail, believe me."

The Chief sat down at his desk and considered. He looked worried.

"So far it's only conjecture," Fernando said, sitting across from the Chief. "Ruby said he was leaving town and mentioned Juarez. That's all we know at the moment. Knowing Jimmy, he could have changed his mind four or five times by now."

"Yeah...I hope. Maybe he'll stop in Cruces and hide out there. Or Carlsbad. Nobody goes to Carlsbad anymore. Too fucking hot."

"If it were me, I'd go to Silver City," Fernando said. "Lotta places to hide out in the Gila."

The Chief leaned back in his chair. "Okay, we have an arrest warrant and an APB out on Jimmy. Let's wait until we get some information on his whereabouts and then talk. Shouldn't take more than twenty-four hours."

Leaving, Fernando decided not to approach Antonio about accompanying him to Juarez or wherever Jimmy went. Not yet. He would wait until time was short and then apply pressure. He didn't think Antonio would really turn him down.

Fernando holed up in his office the rest of the afternoon waiting for developments. About 4 p.m. Linda buzzed him saying she'd just received an anonymous call from a woman claiming to be an attendant at a Sunoco gas station in Las Cruces, about 280 miles south of Santa Fe. The woman said a green Subaru matching the description in the APB had stopped for gas there a few minutes earlier and then driven off, heading south on I-25.

"The woman said she wrote down the license plate number and then checked the APB," Linda added. "She said they matched."

"Okay, Las Cruces is only forty miles from Jaurez. He's probably at the border now."

"So what's the plan?" she asked.

He laughed. "Good question. I guess I'll go home and pack a bag, get ready to head down to Jaurez as soon as we get a fix on a location down there."

"Don't forget your passport," Linda said. "They won't let you cross the border without one. It ain't like it used to be when we were kids. Remember?"

Memories flooded over him, memories of Linda and him at the hotel in Jaurez when they were in their late twenties. Drinking Modelo at the Mercado and having unprotected sex on the hotel patio, eating at the loud café with the sombreros hanging from the ceiling and the mariachis playing fast and furious. Their weekend fling had been his only indiscretion in nearly forty years of married life. Estelle gave him one more chance, just one. He'd walked the line ever since.

He broke the silence. "I remember, Linda. Everything."

She spoke softer now, not her usual dry sarcastic voice. "I don't regret anything, Fernando. Never did."

"You're right. We were just kids."

"We knew what we were doing," she said, still waiting for him to say it.

An image of Linda naked on their chaise lounge flashed through his mind. "I don't regret it either."

The line went dead.

Rattled, overcome by memories of the past, he buzzed Antonio and proposed going for a cold beer at La Fonda Bar. He needed to get his mind off Juarez. Antonio gave his usual response: "Sure, if you're buying."

They met out front of the station and walked across the Plaza to the corner of San Francisco Street. The historic La Fonda, an old Harvey Hotel from the 1920s, looked positively jammed with a line of tourists checking in and others already roaming the halls. A few early drinkers hunkered down at the bar jawing and glancing up at the television above the bar. The bartender saw them come in and pointed to a side table along the wall, away from the crowd.

Tommy came right over and said, "Haven't seen you guys in a while. Thought you might have gone on the wagon."

Antonio laughed. "Fat chance."

"Give us a couple of Modelo drafts," Fernando said.

"You got it."

After Tommy left, Antonio glanced at him and said, "I suppose you're going to try to convince me to go with you to Juarez?"

"I plan to keep buying you beers until you agree. I don't care how many beers it takes, we're not walking out of here until you agree."

Antonio pretended to check his watch. "Okay with me, I don't have anyone waiting for me back at my cabin in the Pecos. Just a wild dog that comes up every evening for a bite to eat and a mangy mountain lion that goes through my trash every so often. Hell, I can check into La Fonda tonight."

Fernando laughed. Then he got serious for a moment. "I'll need back up down there."

"Hah! You'll need a fucking SWAT team. And you'll still be outgunned."

Tommy brought their beers and set them down on the table.

Antonio took a long drink from his mug and smiled.

Fernando did the same. "Is that a yes?"

17

Fernando told Estelle over breakfast the next morning that he might have to go to Juarez to bring Jimmy back. Needless to say she didn't approve of the idea and tried to talk him out of going, but he reminded her that the trip wasn't definite yet, just a possibility. And if he did go, he would take Antonio along for support and return as quickly as possible with or without Jimmy.

He took his second cup of coffee into the bedroom to pack his suitcase, a small carry-on he took whenever he left town for any length of time. All he needed was a shaving kit and a change of clothes and an extra pair of shoes. He wanted to be ready if and when Jimmy surfaced in Juarez.

On the way to the station he stopped at a bank ATM and withdrew some cash. He couldn't think of anything else he needed to do. Like him, Antonio had agreed to have his suitcase packed and ready in his Jeep, so that if the call came, they could leave immediately. It was a good five or six hour drive to Juarez and then you had to make it through customs, although getting in was always a damned sight easier than getting out of Mexico.

The morning became a waiting game. He busied himself with paperwork, trying to keep up. There were always more reports that needed to be completed. At noon he walked next door to the Great Burrito Company and bought a sandwich and cup of coffee with extra cream and sugar.

Linda greeted him at the front desk as soon as he stepped through the front door of the station. "You just missed a call, Fernando. A Deputy

Taggart from Rio Arriba County wants you to call him back. Here's his number."

She handed him a slip of paper.

Taggart? The name didn't ring a bell at first, but then he remembered the officer at Ghost Ranch investigating the vandalism at Casa del Sol. "Did he say what he wanted?"

"Just that he needed some information."

He hurried back to his office and ate lunch quickly. What information could Taggart want from him? Maybe what he and Antonio were doing at Casa del Sol? He never had an opportunity to tell him about Jimmy and their investigation. That would be a problem. He didn't have anything against Taggart, but he wanted to avoid involving the Rio Arriba County Sherriff's Office, which had a bad reputation among lawmen. Let's just say they were not the most professional of crews. They spent as much time fighting among themselves and arresting each other as they did dealing with bad guys. No thanks.

Getting his story straight, he dialed Taggart's number and waited.

"Taggart here," came the response.

Fernando identified himself.

"Detective Lopez, I could use your help. We've had a string of break-ins up here in Abiquiu. I remember seeing you at Ghost Ranch after Casa del Sol was vandalized and...well, we've had another break-in, this one at the main O'Keeffe house in Abiquiu. It doesn't make a bit of sense to me, because nothing was taken from either house. Up here the damned fool broke into O'Keeffe's bomb shelter out back. The house itself wasn't touched, just the bomb shelter. Go figure."

"Really? I didn't even know O'Keeffe had a bomb shelter," was all Fernando could think to say.

"Yeah, I guess it's one of those fallout shelters rich people were building in the fifties and early sixties, back when folks worried about nuclear war," Taggart said.

"Was anything stolen?"

"Not that we can tell. But here's why I'm calling. Why were you at Casa del Sol? Do you know something we don't know about what's going on here?"

Fernando hesitated. "We were chasing a murder suspect, a guy named Jimmy Mackey wanted for the murder of a Santa Fe woman. He'd been at Ghost Ranch the day before."

"Okay...but could this be the guy who's vandalizing the O'Keeffe houses?" Taggart asked.

"Could be," Fernando said, trying to decide whether to tell Taggart the tall-tale of Georgia O'Keeffe's hidden painting.

"Well, why would he vandalize two of her houses?" Taggart laughed. "Does he not like her paintings or something?"

Fernando bit the bullet and told Taggart what Ruby had said about the missing O'Keeffe painting that some people believed was hidden in one of her houses, an apocalyptic painting she didn't want public until after her death.

"Sounds like horseshit to me."

"Probably, but Jimmy might be working with a gallery owner trying to find the painting," Fernando said.

"Sounds like that boy has more legal problems than he can shake a stick at."

"If we can ever find him," Fernando added.

Taggart paused for a long moment. "Can you come take a look at this? Might give you some clues. Looks like he camped in the bomb shelter last night. There's an empty bottle of vodka here and a bunch of food wrappers. Plus one of those little propane canisters camping stoves use nowadays. And I can see the imprint of a mat or a sleeping bag on the floor of the shelter. It's pretty damn dusty in here. You can almost trace the movements he made by looking at the dust."

Fernando sighed, thinking about the repercussions of what he had just learned. "I'll be there in about an hour. Can you wait?"

"Look for me in the parking lot," Taggart said. "I'll be in my car."

So much for Juarez. If jimmy spent the night in Abiquiu, he for damned sure couldn't have been seen in Las Cruces late yesterday afternoon. The call must have been an attempt to get him off Jimmy's trail. Sounded like something Ruby would pull to protect her ex-husband. Just what kind of sick, preternatural bond did Ruby have with Jimmy that could survive marriage and divorce and whatever perverse relationship the two of them had today? Didn't make any sense to him. If you were divorced, you were divorced. Enough said.

Antonio would be happy to know they weren't going to Juarez. On the other hand the Chief might be pissed, because without Juarez they had no leads on Jimmy's whereabouts.

Where could he have gone from Abiquiu? The fact that he had camping equipment meant he could camp anywhere in the mountains of northern New Mexico from Santa Fe to the Colorado state line. But Jimmy didn't strike him as a long-term camper.

Knowing Jimmy, he would look for a place where he could find sympathetic souls. For Jimmy that meant an art community. He would also look for a place where he could find a dependable supply of liquor. That meant a city. Where was the largest art community in northern New Mexico outside Santa Fe?

That would be Taos, a mere fifty miles from Abiquiu going through El Rito and Ojo Caliente. Taos made more sense than Juarez. Taos was the last refuge of the hippies who invaded the area in the 1970s, when Dennis Hopper was king and the wild weed was cheap.

Antonio would be a happy man.

18

"Abiquiu?" I thought we were going to Juarez? Antonio dropped his suitcase on the office floor.

"Change of plan," Fernando said. "Looks like Ruby tried to send us on a wild goose chase to protect Jimmy. I'll explain in the car."

"The lyin' bitch."

"Leave your suitcase here. You may need it later."

With that, they hurried out of the station and retraced their steps to Abiquiu, following Highway 84 through Española to the ancient village built on top of a mesa. At the Abiquiu road sign he turned left and climbed the curving road up to a dirt plaza. Once at the top he saw the O'Keeffe house straight ahead, partially hidden behind an adobe wall. The one-story sprawling house overlooked the highway below. The parking area turned out to be on the far side of the house. He pulled into the gravel driveway and parked behind the sheriff's cruiser.

Taggart sat inside the cruiser with his driver's side door wide open listening to his radio. When he heard their car, he checked in his rear view mirror and then stepped gingerly out of the vehicle. A big man with a red face and dark sunglasses, he walked arthritically over to meet them. A toothpick dangled from his mouth.

Taggart checked his watch. "Well, you boys are pretty near on time. Let me show you the bomb shelter and then you can tell me what the hell's going on around here."

They followed him down a hill behind the house to what looked like a bunker dug out of the hillside. Rocks layered the front of the bunker, as well as the roof. A steel door hung wide open, the locking mechanism damaged by a heavy crowbar. As they edged up to the bunker they saw its dark interior, with a streak of light slashing across the concrete floor. The small chamber reeked of that dank, moldy smell common to wet basements--or caves.

Fernando's eyes adjusted slowly to the darkness. He could see cabinets thrown open along the back wall and piles of canned food and medical supplies spilled on the floor. Someone, no doubt Jimmy, had taken a pickaxe or crowbar and ripped out the wooden back of the cabinets, revealing the concrete wall underneath. Along the left wall stood a small wooden table and two canvas chairs, with two lanterns placed under the table. On the right a canvas cot had been pushed up against the wall. The canvas was torn and sagging on the dusty concrete floor. Everything inside the shelter was covered by dust and cobwebs.

"This is how we found it," Taggart said. He pointed to the broken cot. "You can see how the canvas ripped when he tried to sleep on the cot. So then he set up his sleeping mat on the floor back here by the shelves."

Antonio examined the canvas chair. The canvas ripped as soon as he pushed on it.

Taggart stepped over to the table. "He must be pretty well equipped for camping.
Over there's the empty propane canister. You know, the small ones used with Coleman camping stoves."

Fernando wasn't listening to Taggart. Instead he sorted through a pile of trash the intruder had discarded. Cans and food wrappers and what looked like the bottle of vodka they saw in Jimmy's cabin back at Ghost Ranch, empty now. And something else. Several sheets of wadded up drawing paper. He opened them one at a time and spread them out on the table. They were colored pencil sketches of the Abiquiu landscape.

He took one of the sketches outside and found that it matched the view from the door of the bunker: cottonwood trees and the Chama River foregrounded against a background of pink, gray, and yellow mesas. The other sketches were of the same view seen from slightly different angles. Typical of Jimmy's landscapes, lots of colors for the tourists.

"What do you think?" Taggart asked.

Fernando nodded and handed the sketches to Taggart. "Yeah, I think it's our guy. Jimmy Mackey. He paints landscapes. Just like these."

Taggart spit out his toothpick on the floor of the bunker. "Why in hell would he think Georgia O'Keeffe would hide this so-called end-of-the-world painting, even if it did exist, in a damn bomb shelter?"

"Good question. I suppose because not many people know the bomb shelter exists. It would be a safe place to hide it."

Antonio snorted. "Not to mention the fact that Jimmy Mackey is bat-shit crazy."

Taggart nodded. "I can see that. One thing's for damn sure, there's no security alarm in the bomb shelter. And there's no night watchman or anything like that out here in the boondocks."

Fernando picked up the propane canister and shook it to make sure it was empty. "Plus, I think he was looking for a place to spend the night. Where better to hide out than Georgia O'Keeffe's fallout shelter?"

"Wouldn't the neighbors up here have noticed Jimmy's car?" Antonio asked, moving back toward the door.

"We think he parked a block down the road at the Abiquiu Inn," Taggart said. "His car would blend in with the others. Take him five minutes to walk up here."

Antonio started to cough. "This place stinks--it's giving me an asthma attack."

Fernando watched Antonio step out of the bomb shelter and start walking up the hill.

Taggart kept checking his watch, also eager to get going. "The O'Keeffe Museum is sending a locksmith up here to fix the lock. They own the property now. I don't know what the hell's taking so long."

Fernando stayed a few minutes longer, going over every corner of the shelter in case he'd missed something. Finally he gave up and followed Antonio and Taggart up the hill.

Antonio was already in their cruiser, waiting for him. "Let's get the hell out of here. This place gives me the creeps."

Taggart watched them drive off before climbing into his car to wait for the locksmith.

Fernando drove down the bumpy road to the highway and turned right. The Abiquiu Inn came into sight almost immediately. He steered into the main drive and followed a loop that took them around a motel-like building of separate rooms. From there they drove through a stand of cottonwood trees to a line of casitas, each with a separate parking area. He eased along the rock and gravel road, stopping frequently to look in vain for Jimmy's Subaru. The loop then took them across a narrow bridge to the main building, where the office and café were located.

He stopped in front of the office and looked around. "I'll check inside to see if they've seen Jimmy."

Antonio nodded. "I'll walk around the loop and see what I can find."

In the office Fernando found a smartly dressed woman with gray hair and glasses behind the front desk. "Can I help you?" she asked.

He showed the woman his badge. "I'm looking for a man who drives a green Subaru. Jimmy Mackey. He may have parked the Subaru here last night."

"Yes, actually one of our cooks reported a green Subaru parked behind the restaurant last night. He said it was gone by the time he reported for breakfast duty."

Fernando nodded. "Do you have any record of a Jimmy Mackey staying here...or any future reservations under that name?"

She checked her computer, hitting a few keys and scrolling down. "No, nothing under that name. Why, does he drive the green Subaru?"

Fernando nodded. "We're looking for him in connection with a couple of local break-ins."

She looked worried. "Well, I hope you catch him."

"Thank you."

He returned to the car and waited. From there he could see Antonio meandering along the road through the casitas. While he watched, the big man stopped to talk to a maid coming out of the last casita. They chatted for a moment and then the woman pointed toward the office. Finally she returned to her cart and proceeded to the next casita.

Antonio walked across the bridge and up to the parking lot. He signaled with a thumb over his shoulder. "Just talked to a maid down there. She said she saw Jimmy get out of his car last night. Geeky little guy, she described him. Carrying a big bag."

"I got the same thing in the office," Fernando said.

Antonio looked around. "So where's the little sonofabitch going next?"

"I think we both know the person who can answer that."

They didn't have to say the name.

19

They didn't make it back to Santa Fe until after six p.m. They stopped first at Ruby's pottery co-op in the Railyard and found it closed for the day. No one answered when they knocked on the door of her apartment next door. So grasping at straws Fernando suggested they head up to El Farol on Canyon Road. The local artists liked to gather there on Friday afternoons to talk shop and complain about the tourists, who had bad taste and no manners.

Antonio laughed. "Hah! Every night is Friday night for that group. Bunch of drunks."

Fernando parked in the lot across the street and followed Antonio across Canyon Road. A couple of bearded old timers with long white hair sat on the porch watching them approach. Supposedly dating from 1835, relatively new in a city founded in 1610, El Farol looked like a million bucks after its recent remodel. White stucco with brown window frames and a red door, the restaurant opened up into a lively bar where the usual crowd of eccentrics and ne'er-do-wells exchanged tall tales and raunchy jokes. Jimmy's people.

Fernando bypassed the bar and stepped into the restaurant part of El Farol, a larger room with colorful Southwestern décor. He saw Ruby sitting with several other artist types at a corner round table already cluttered with empty beer and wine glasses. The others he didn't immediately recognize, partly because they were engaged in an animated argument about something. An old man with snow white hair, who he now recognized as Wayne Fontenot, said something to Ruby and she responded with: "You're full of shit."

He and Antonio sat down at the table behind Ruby. Everyone at the other table stopped talking. Ruby turned her head slowly and when she saw them launched a string of Spanish obscenities at them.

"Howdy, Ruby," he said.

"What now? Why do you two apes keep bugging me? I told you everything I know about Kim and what happened that night." She opened her arms wide. "What the fuck?"

Antonio's face turned bright red. Not a good sign. "Didn't think we'd be back from Juarez so soon?"

She gave him the finger.

"Yeah, thanks for the Juarez tip, Ruby," Fernando added. "You said you'd give us the truth. Why are you still trying to protect Jimmy? Why are you lying for him?

"Because he's my friend. My ex-husband."

"Hah! All the two of you do is fight," Fernando said.

"Oh fuck you, Fernando. You wouldn't understand...."

He sighed. "You should know that forensics just identified Kim's blood on some of Jimmy's clothes. An arrest warrant has been issued."

She seemed taken aback. "But Jimmy didn't have any reason to kill her. He didn't have a motive. They were good friends. They were sleeping together."

Fernando stood up and leaned over her. "Come on, Ruby, where is he? Help us find him. If he's innocent, he has nothing to worry about."

Ruby shook her head. "I don't know. I really don't. He has lots of friends in northern New Mexico, especially in El Rito and Taos. He wouldn't tell me where he was going, but my guess is that he's somewhere around Taos."

He stood up straight. "Okay, Ruby, but tell me the truth. I'm trying to help Jimmy, but I can't do that unless I find him. Down at the station they're ready to charge him with murder."

"I'm telling you the truth," she said. "Taos is my best guess. I can give you the names of some of his friends there, at least the ones I know about. That would be a place to start. I'll call you tomorrow morning."

"Thanks, that'll help."

He started to walk away, but she reached out and grabbed his arm. "Fernando, don't hurt him. He's just an overgrown kid. He's harmless."

He nodded and walked away. He heard Antonio's footsteps close behind. When they stepped out into the cool evening Antonio asked, "What do you think?"

"Sounds more plausible than Juarez," Fernando said.

"Hah! That's not saying much."

They drove back down to the Washington Avenue station in silence. At the station parking lot he dropped off Antonio and exchanged their cruiser for his Plymouth. Then he drove back around on the Paseo to Acequia Madre and home.

Estelle had already eaten. His dinner sat on the table, cold.

"You better heat that up!" she yelled from the living room. He could hear the nightly PBS news on the television. Estelle didn't like to miss the PBS news.

He warmed his meal in the microwave and sat down to eat. Before he could start Estelle popped into the kitchen.

"By the way, Laura Aragon called from the mayor's office. She wants you to call back. I wrote down her number on the pad."

He hadn't heard from Laura, an old acquaintance, for several months. She worked in the mayor's office as one of two budget managers.

So after he finished his dinner he dialed her number.

"Fernando. Thanks for calling back," she said. "Haven't talked to you in a while. Where you been?"

"Actually I've been on medical leave pending retirement for the past two months. I broke a couple of ribs and hurt my shoulder in a jeep accident at Chaco Canyon. The Chief asked me to come back for the Kim Martin case."

"Yeah, that's why I'm calling," she said quietly. He picked up a dark, somber tone in her voice.

She continued, almost whispering. "Something happened at the office the day Kim was murdered. I should have called you earlier, but I was scared. I didn't want to lose my job."

"I understand," he said, "but don't worry about retaliation. Anything you tell me will be kept confidential."

Laura paused. "I'm embarrassed by having to talk about this sort of thing, but I thought it was important for you to know. Like I said, this happened on the day Kim was murdered. Kim came into the office early that morning. I don't know where she'd been. She looked sort of rumpled, like she'd just gotten out of bed. Anyway, she and Joe started arguing. The door to the office was closed, but I could hear them shouting. Some nasty things were said by both of them."

"Like what?" Fernando asked.

"Well, he called her an f'ing slut. That kind of thing. She screamed he wasn't a real man, that he was a lousy husband and lover. That he didn't know how to satisfy a woman. Ugly. Very ugly."

"Sounds like it."

"Then he slapped her. I could hear it through the door. Kim screamed and ran out of the office crying and holding her face. I could see her running down the hall from my desk. I stood up and went into the hallway intending to help her. Comfort her, whatever I could do. But then I saw Joe standing there. He gave me a dirty look, so I went back into my office and didn't say anything. I was afraid to get involved, you know?"

"I do. Had he hit her before?"

"Not to my knowledge," Laura said. "They'd had fights before, but none as violent as this one."

"But if this was happening at work, you have to wonder what was going on at home," Fernando said.

Dead silence at the other end. Then she said, "I really hate to tattle on Joe...you know, to get involved in this kind of stuff...but I thought you should know."

"I should. You did the right thing, Laura."

20

Fernando arrived at the station early. He'd arranged to meet the Mayor first thing that morning. So he parked in his usual spot in the parking lot and then walked down Marcy Street to Lincoln Avenue. Just as he reached the intersection his cell phone rang. It turned out to be Ruby calling with the names of Jimmy's friends in Taos. He took a seat on the nearest bench. The morning sun and the fresh alpine air invigorated him as he listened to Ruby.

"Go ahead," he said, once he had his notebook in hand.

"Okay, here's a list. Jimmy's a good friend of the Artists Co-op owner on the Plaza. I think his name is Tomas Alvarez. He's also friends with the owners of Red Dog Brewery about a mile north on Paseo del Pueblo Norte. Bill and Mary something or other. Then there's Richard Romero, the owner of Taos Mercantile and Livery on Mabel Dodge Lane. That's also off Paseo del Pueblo Norte, just after Red Dog Brewery. And finally there's Jimmy's ex-wife, Lauren Mackey in Arroyo Hondo. She owns Arroyo Hondo Arts, which is back in the hills off Highway five twenty-two. You know, the road to Questa. She does tie-dye and some weaving."

"That's it?"

"If Jimmy's in Taos, he's contacted at least one of them, probably more," Ruby said. "I'm positive. He's known all of them for over twenty years, ever since he lived there in the nineties. That's where he learned to paint. At the Taos Art School."

"What kind of relationship does he have with Lauren? I assume he's still in contact with her."

"Hah! The same kind of relationship he has with me. We hate the lying, cheating bastard, but we also love him and want to protect him. It's complicated. You wouldn't understand because you're a guy."

"I guess not...." Fernando said.

He sat on the bench for a few minutes collecting his thoughts and planning the logistics of a quick trip to Taos, which would be a lot easier than going down to Juarez and having to deal with customs and the cartels.

He checked his watch and cursed. He was already late for a nine a.m. meeting with the Mayor.

Fernando hurried over to city hall and found Joe Martin waiting in his office, his door wide open. His bodyguard was nowhere in sight. In fact, the entire suite of rooms looked deserted except for Martin.

"Mr. Mayor," he said, walking into the office. "Thanks again for meeting with me."

Martin nodded from one of two leather chairs next to a bay window. "Have a seat, Fernando," he said, pointing to the other chair.

He sat facing Martin.

"So tell me, what's new in the investigation?" Martin asked. "Do you have Jimmy Mackey in custody?"

"No. We think he's in Taos. Maybe hiding out with friends."

"Then why aren't you in Taos?" Martin asked.

"We're on our way."

"Why is it taking so long? He's a murderer and needs to be behind bars."

Fernando frowned. "Well, he hasn't been convicted yet. Innocent until proven guilty, right?"

"I don't give a damn about his rights. He's a murderer. They found Kim's blood on his clothing. What more do you need?"

Fernando held his tongue.

"So what did you want to talk to me about? You said you had some questions?"

"I do. Sensitive questions. But I need to ask them."

"What do you mean?" Martin looked uncomfortable.

"We have a report by a witness that you and Kim argued in your office the day Kim was murdered. An argument that turned violent when you struck her across the face. She was seen running out of your office crying, holding her face."

Martin's face turned red. "Are you suggesting I murdered my wife?"

"I'm not suggesting anything," Fernando said. "I'm asking you why you and Kim argued and why you assaulted her."

"Assault? Oh come on, I didn't assault her. We had an argument, like most divorcing couples. We raised our voices. So what?"

"So why did you hit her?" Fernando shot back.

"Look. We said some nasty personal things about each other. I think you can imagine what those things were from our previous conversation. I may have touched her, but nothing more than that."

Fernando nodded. "Apparently that was enough to send her running out of the room crying."

"Let me put it this way. She got what she deserved," Martin said.

"Had you hit her before?"

"What?"

"How often did you hit her? Every time you argued?"

Martin's face turned fiery red. "Goddamnit! I don't like what you're insinuating."

"You didn't answer my question," Fernando said.

For a brief moment Martin seemed ready to jump out of his seat and get physical, but he quickly brought his emotions under control.

Sitting there Fernando realized how much he disliked Martin, a pompous ass with a bad temper hiding behind his laid-back Santa Fe chic. Underneath the easy-going attitude Martin could be a mean sonofabitch, especially to women. With men he would be a fucking coward, like all wife beaters.

"Let me remind you of something, Fernando, just in case you've forgotten," Martin said, modulating his voice.

Fernando knew what was coming next.

"Remember, I'm a powerful man in this city. I can do a lot of damage to a man's career. Do you understand what I'm saying?"

"As clear as day," Fernando said.

"Now you get the hell out of my office and go find Jimmy Mackey. I want him locked up and charged with the murder of my wife. No more fucking around. You know he did it, so arrest him."

Fernando stood and without responding walked out of the office and exited city hall.

21

They took the low road to Taos. Highway 68 ran alongside the Rio Grande. The river looked even lower than it usually did in September. No doubt about it, water seemed to get scarcer every year in the Southwest. Approaching Velarde they could see kayakers and white water rafters in the shallow river. He slowed down to take a closer look, pissing off a motorcyclist tailgating him. The hotshot gave them the finger as he raced past. He checked the rearview mirror to make sure there were no other speedsters wanting to pass but saw only an olive colored van also slowing down to take a look at the activity on the river.

Minutes later they crested the last hill and drove by the Ranchos de Taos church, famously painted and photographed by more artists than he could count. The highway stretched out as far as the eye could see, with Taos sprawled on either side of the highway and the 13,000-foot peaks of the Taos Ski Basin straight ahead. He ignored the fast food restaurants and the other commercial claptrap and drove into the heart of the old city, turning left into the historic Plaza area. He parked at a meter in front of the Hotel La Fonda de Taos and walked to the Artists Co-op on the opposite corner of the Plaza.

Rounding the corner he saw a man painting outside the co-op. The man stood in front of an easel holding a palette splotched with colors and painting with a long brush. Wearing a wide-brim sunhat and a sweaty kerchief around his neck, the man looked the part of a western artist. He had a brown weathered face, crinkly eyes, and a pointed goatee gone white with age. He stood back from the easel when he saw them approaching and said, "Howdy."

"Howdy," Antonio responded, glancing at a half-finished abstract of the Taos mountains.

Fernando stepped up beside Antonio. "We're looking for an artist named Jimmy Mackey. Do you know him?"

"Mackey? No, I don't recall anyone by that name."

He turned and walked inside the co-op, leaving Antonio talking to the cowboy painter. Inside he made his way through the counters and around the walls covered with bright paintings to a desk in back, where a tall, emaciated man with a clean-shaven face stood watching him approach. He wore jeans and a blue denim shirt and looked to be in his late fifties, with salt and pepper hair and dark bags under his eyes. He didn't look well.

"Can I help you?" the man asked, his eyelids half closed.

"I'm looking for an artist named Jimmy Mackey. Do you know him?"

The man opened his eyes wider. "He lives in Santa Fe."

"I know, but I think he may be in Taos visiting," Fernando said.

"Yeah? Well, I haven't seen him since this last Spring when he came up for the Taos Art Fair. If you see him, tell him he still owes me money, will you?"

Fernando laughed. "Apparently he owes a lot of people money."

"I'm not surprised. He doesn't sell much these days. His landscapes are commonplace...platitudes, really. His Chopped Nudes are better, but they only appeal to a select audience. Every time I see him he hits me up for money."

"Do you sell any of his paintings here?" Fernando asked.

"Not any more. As I say, they don't sell. We had a Chopped Nude here a few years back. Took years to sell the painting. Finally some rich Hollywood dude with a ranch outside of town bought it for half of what Jimmy wanted. No more, thanks."

"Does Jimmy sell at any of the other galleries in Taos?"

The man shook his head. "Not to my knowledge. He has a bad reputation. He drinks a lot and causes trouble. And like I said, his paintings don't sell. There's just too much competition these days."

"Okay. Much obliged."

Back outside Fernando was surprised to find Antonio and the cowboy painter discussing abstract art. Antonio didn't like it, the cowboy did. He listened to them argue for a few seconds and then turned and walked away. Eventually he heard Antonio following along behind.

Crossing the Plaza Fernando saw what looked like the same olive colored van that was behind them on the highway into town. Turned out to be an old Ford Expedition, a real gas guzzler.

When they reached their unmarked squad car Fernando turned to Antonio and said, "I didn't know you were an art critic."

"Hah! I'm not. I just want to be able to recognize what I'm looking at, you know what I mean."

He climbed into the squad car and slammed the door. "Where next? Red Dog Brewery or Taos Mercantile?"

Antonio checked his watch. "Oh, hell, let's do Red Dog first. It's close enough to happy hour. I could use a beer."

So they drove up Paseo del Pueblo Norte to Red Dog Brewery, a funky frame building with a large outdoor patio under a catchy sign that featured a big red dog drinking from a mug of beer. The parking lot was crowded with several trucks and trailers carrying kayaks and river rafts, a common sight in Taos where river-boating was one of the main industries. He pulled into a tight parking space at the end of the lot and turned to Antonio. "Only one beer."

Antonio's capacity for alcohol was legendary. Fernando's wasn't.

Inside they found a couple of old timers sitting at the bar nursing their beers, while groups of young kayakers and rafters crowded around the tables out on the patio. The young people, laughing loudly, seemed to be celebrating something, maybe the end of the river-boating season since it was already late September. Whatever it was, the petite woman behind the bar didn't look happy about it. She came over to greet them as soon as they took seats at the bar.

"Sorry about the noise," she said, brushing a strand of gray hair out of her eyes. "What can I get you fellows?"

"No problem," Fernando said. "Are you Mary, by any chance?" he asked.

She smiled. "How did you know my name?"

"Ruby Montez told us to stop by. We're looking for Jimmy Mackey, an old friend of ours. Have you seen him?"

"Jimmy? Yeah, he came in yesterday afternoon for a couple of beers. Didn't pay for them, of course. Jimmy never does. We call him Good Time Jimmy. Always wants to party, never wants to pay."

"Sounds like Jimmy. Did he say where he was staying?"

She shook her head. "He said he was heading up North. I don't know if he meant Arroyo Hondo, where his ex-wife lives, or all the way to Durango."

"Why Durango?" Fernando asked.

"Sure. A gallery up there next to the Strater Hotel shows his work, or at least used to. He's pretty talented, you know."

"Yes, he is."

"So what can I get you?" she asked again.

"Give us a couple of Dos Equis drafts," Antonio said, taking charge.

While she drew the beers Fernando asked, "How well do you know Lauren Mackey?"

"Well enough," she said and set the foaming beers on the bar. "She comes in on occasion."

"Are she and Jimmy still friendly?"

"Yeah, they're still friends. Jimmy's a sweetheart...when he's not drinking."

Antonio laughed. "When's that?"

She gave Antonio a nasty look and moved off down the bar to serve the old timers.

Later, after a second round, Fernando finally managed to get Antonio out of the Red Dog. When they were in the car Antonio said, "Is it just my imagination, or were those glasses exceptionally small?"

"It's definitely your imagination."

With that he drove on down the Paseo looking for Taos Mercantile and Livery. He knew he'd found it when he saw bales of hay and bags of livestock feed stacked high along the road. He pulled into a gravel parking lot lined with small tractors and other farm equipment. Inside the store was no less crowded, with aisles of garden implements and power tools and construction supplies. A short, stocky man wearing a Ski Taos T-shirt stood at the front counter watching them enter.

"Afternoon," the man said.

"Afternoon," Fernando responded. "We're looking for a friend of ours, Jimmy Mackey. We hear he's in town visiting. Have you seen him?"

"Hah! Not likely He owes me too much money. He may never show his face in here again because he knows I'll want to collect."

"That right?"

The man nodded. "I like Jimmy, but he never pays for anything, he just borrows. How the hell does a man get through life like that?"

"His ex-wives tell me it's because all the women like him and want to take care of him," Fernando said.

The man laughed and said, "More power to him, I guess. I just wish I could get some of my money back."

"Good luck with that," Antonio said.

The man shook his head sadly as they walked outside into the late afternoon sun. Only a couple hours of sunlight remained.

It was time to make a plan.

22

"What? You wanna stay here? You're telling me this is all the Santa Fe Police Department can afford?" Antonio asked.

"What are you complaining about? You live in a cabin at the edge of the national forest," Fernando pointed out.

"Even my cabin is better than this dump."

Fernando looked over the El Pueblo, a 1960s motel with small rooms and old furniture and wondered. Still, the motor lodge did have its charm, mainly its proximity to the famous Taos Pueblo, a World Heritage Site. Not to mention its hot-tub-sized pool where an unruly throng of out-of-staters fought for space to insert their bloated white bodies. Overhead a neon sign blinked on and off in the dying afternoon light. Maybe about Midnight the crowd at the pool would thin out enough for a person to sink his entire body in the bubbling chlorinated water.

"Let's go, before it starts to get dark," he said.

They tossed their bags on the beds and climbed back in the squad car. This time he followed the Paseo out of town to the Highway 522 intersection and turned left. Ten miles up the highway he entered Arroyo Hondo, not much more than a scattering of adobes and small farms set back from the road. Fernando stopped at the only gas station in town and asked the attendant for directions to Lauren Mackey's house. The attendant told him to take Rio Hondo Road west to an unmarked dirt road and turn left. He would see Lauren's farm straight ahead on the right side of the road. If he missed the turnoff he would eventually come to the hot springs along the Rio Grande. The river meant he'd gone too far.

Antonio was skeptical. "How do we tell which unmarked dirt road is the one we want?"

Fernando ignored Antonio's questions and drove up the highway to

Rio Hondo Road, a primitive gravel road that curved westward. The car kicked up a cloud of dust as he proceeded slowly toward the river looking for an unmarked dirt road off to the left. He stopped first at what turned out to be a goat path and then again at a dry arroyo that crossed over the road. The third stop turned out to be the unmarked road. As soon as he turned left he saw the farm up ahead: a sprawling adobe house and several outbuildings. He quickly turned around and headed back to Rio Hondo Road.

Antonio, confused, asked, "Where are you going?"

"Let's go up a ways and see if we can find higher ground. You know, stake out the place for a while and look for any sign of Jimmy. I don't want to rush in and risk losing him again."

That seemed to satisfy Antonio.

The further Fernando drove, the rougher the road became. Finally he found himself stopping and starting, easing over deep ruts and around exposed rocks. The road rose slightly as it approached the river, as he hoped. They came finally to a dirt parking area where a crude sign marked a path to a hot springs along the river. The path ran though a stand of boulders. He pulled off onto the mesa and parked behind an outcropping of rock that jutted out from the river. There the car could not be seen from the road or the parking area.

Fernando grabbed his binoculars from the glove compartment and followed Antonio back to the parking area. They climbed up on a ledge of rock and took shelter behind one large boulder, from where they looked down on Lauren Mackey's farm. Below them the farm spread out over a flat area of grassland, much larger than it looked from the road. It included an orchard and what looked like a large commercial garden. A small tractor and flatbed truck were parked near the garden, but there was no sign of Jimmy's green Subaru.

Using the binoculars, Fernando scanned the adobe house and the smaller buildings looking for human activity. He saw one woman with a basket, presumably Lauren Mackey, gathering tomatoes and green chile in the garden. She wore a straw hat and gloves and heavy clothing. She took her time walking among the rows, picking the ripest vegetables. When she finished she carried the basket back to a patio behind the house and sat in a reclining chair. Then she took a number out of her shirt pocket and lit it with a lighter, inhaling deeply. She sat there smoking, gazing up at the hill where they crouched hidden from her sight. Meditating or daydreaming or whatever people did while smoking. It had been so long since he'd smoked weed that he could no longer remember.

"What do you see?" Antonio asked.

"Must be Lauren down there on the patio. I don't see Jimmy's car or any sign of him."

He looked around the farm for places where Jimmy might hide the Subaru. Maybe inside one of the larger sheds. That was one possibility. Or maybe down the road behind a hill.

"What's that white shape behind the trees?" Antonio pointed to a corner of the orchard.

Fernando trained his binoculars on the white object, which turned out to be the top of a canvas teepee. He could tell by the poles that crisscrossed over the canvas.

"Looks like a teepee."

Antonio nodded. "This would be a good place for Jimmy to hide out...if he could ditch his car."

"There's no place to hide it down there," Fernando said. "It would have to be down the road somewhere."

Antonio laughed. "Old Jimmy must be quite the ladies man to have all these women looking after him. I don't get what they see in that little prick."

"Mystery to me," Fernando mumbled, scanning the driveway. He saw an old Chevy pickup and a Toyota Prius side by side.

By Northern New Mexico standards, Lauren Mackey looked fairly prosperous, more prosperous than Jimmy.

The sun slowly sank behind the western horizon as they watched. The eastern sky darkened, plunging the farm into shadows. Eventually the woman on the patio carried her basket into the house. They waited for a few minutes to see if Jimmy or his Subaru would appear. Neither did. It was time to call it quits. Maybe tomorrow they would have better luck.

Fernando turned to Antonio. "Let's come back tomorrow early and watch the place. If he doesn't show, we'll walk down after dark and search the outbuildings. And the teepee."

Fernando led the way, walking back to the parking area where a group of young people pulled up in their VW Vanagon. The doors flew open and four people jumped out of the van, two men and two women.

All of them stripped off their clothes, totally ignoring him and Antonio. Then they ran off bare-assed naked toward the hot springs, their junk jiggling as they ran.

Suddenly one of the young women stopped and turned to face the two of them. Drop-dead gorgeous, she had long black hair hanging over her breasts and big eyes. "Hey–you guys want to join us?"

"I wish," Fernando said.

Antonio just stared.

"Suit yourself," she said, and jogged off to find her friends.

23

Fernando woke up with an aching back and a bad attitude as soon as he remembered where he was: on a sagging mattress at El Pueblo Motor Lodge. He was tired of chasing Jimmy around Northern New Mexico and sorry he'd come out of retirement. He missed his quiet home on Acequia Madre. The world could go to hell as far as he was concerned. All he wanted from life, what time he had left, was his quiet corner of Santa Fe.

He saw no sign of Antonio until he glanced out the window and saw the burly ex-Marine doing jumping jacks in the parking lot. Then the big man took off jogging God knows where. What was wrong with people who exercised first thing in the morning?

Grumbling to himself, he fumbled with the automatic coffee maker on the counter. The coffee improved his mood. At least he could think clearly. He would give this one more day. If Jimmy didn't turn up at his ex-wife's farm in Arroyo Hondo by nightfall, he was heading back to Santa Fe and saying to hell with it. Chief could give the case to Manny and let him chase Jimmy for a while. Maybe Manny's sense of humor was what this case needed. He'd gone to the dark place and frankly didn't give a damn what happened to any of them.

About half an hour later Antonio came back hot and covered with sweat.

Fernando drank another cup of coffee while Antonio took a quick shower and then they walked down the street to Michael's Kitchen for breakfast. He asked for eggs and toast, while Antonio ordered Huevos Rancheros with side orders of bacon, sausage, and ham. When their food arrived, he had to sit there and watch Antonio shovel in one spoonful of food after another like an old-fashioned fireman on a train shoveling coal into the engine. It was truly depressing.

"Damn! You eat like a pig," he said finally.

Antonio wiped his mouth with a napkin. "I'm a big man. I get hungry."

Just as they finished their last cup of coffee his cell phone rang. "Now what?" he asked out loud.

"Fernando, this is Linda calling from the station. I got some bad news. The Taos County Sheriff just found Jimmy's car parked just off the Rio Grande Gorge Bridge. Do you know where the bridge is located?"

"Of course. Who doesn't?"

"On Highway sixty-four west of Taos. You better check it out right away. They think the car has been parked there overnight."

Now he understood her meaning. The bridge spanned the wide Rio Grand Gorge 650 feel above the river. Though the river above and below the bridge was famous for kayaking and other white water activities, the bridge itself was famous for one thing and one thing only: suicide. Every year five to ten people committed suicide by jumping off the bridge and falling on the rocks below. To his knowledge no one ever survived jumping off the Rio Grande Gorge Bridge.

If Jimmy's car had been there overnight, there was a better than average chance he'd climbed up on the bridge railing and taken the easy way out. The coward. The fucking coward!

Fernando sighed. "Got you."

There was a pause at the other end of the line. Then Linda said, "Maybe it's for the best, Fernando."

"No...I don't believe anything's ever 'for the best.' We'll check it out and get back to you." He ended the call.

Antonio understood. He didn't have to explain.

He counted out a pile of ten-dollar bills and left them on the table. They walked back to the motel without speaking. They stopped in the parking lot before going in to the room.

"What do you think? Should I extend the reservation for tonight?" Fernando asked.

"I suppose," Antonio said. "I mean, it'll take them a while to find and bring up the body."

So Fernando went to the office and re-upped for another night. The lady at the counter gave him a multiple night discount since it was past the tourist season and guests were in short supply. "Maybe tomorrow too?" she asked, smiling.

"I hope not," he replied, walking out of the office.

He found Antonio already in the cruiser. He joined the big man and hit the ignition. They followed Paseo del Pueblo Norte to Highway 64 West, coming to the Rio Grande Gorge Bridge in a matter of minutes.

Out here the Rio Grande had cut a deep jagged channel out of the flat mesa. The gorge took your breath away when you first approached the bridge and saw the open mesa fall away and plunge two hundred yards to the river. The bridge afforded a spectacular view of the winding river below and of the mountain ranges that surrounded the mesa. It was a place of beauty and death inhabited by more ghosts than anyone cared to count or remember.

He pulled up and parked on the side of the highway directly behind the Taos County Sherriff's car. Jimmy's green Subaru sat idle in the small parking area off to the side of the bridge.

A young muscular Sherriff met them in the parking lot. His badge read "Anthony Padilla." "Are you the detective from Santa Fe?" he asked as they walked up.

"Yes, Fernando Lopez," he introduced himself. "This is Sergeant Antonio Blake. We've been chasing this guy for a couple of days. When did you discover the car?"

"Last night about ten o'clock someone called in to report it. Looked suspicious because there was no sign of the driver. You know what that usually means. So we came back this morning and found it still here. That's when we called your station."

"We appreciate the call," Fernando said.

"Let me show you what we found."

Padilla led them over to Jimmy's Subaru. He opened the driver's side door and pointed to the seat. "There's the note he left."

He reached in and grabbed the paper, a handwritten note scribbled on a brown paper bag: "My last will and testimony: I leave all my belongings, including my studio, to Ruby Montez." It was signed "Jimmy C. Mackey."

Fernando handed the note to Antonio who looked it over and handed it back. He returned the note to Padilla and then looked in the back of the SUV. He saw the duffel bag containing the tools Jimmy had used at Ghost Ranch, but no suitcase or backpack with Jimmy's clothes. Other than the duffel bag and the note, the Subaru was empty.

"Everything all right?" Padilla asked, noticing his concern.

"Yeah...so what's next?"

"We called the Search and Rescue Team this morning. They should be here by noon. They have to put in from a landing a few miles up river at El Prado and then come down the rapids. Thing is, it could take a day or two to find the body. The current's strong right now, so there's no telling how far down the river they'll have to search. Usually doesn't take more than a couple of days, though. Can you guys stay in Taos that long?"

He looked at Antonio. Antonio looked at him.

"Sure," he said. "Whatever it takes.

24

The Search and Rescue team didn't arrive until after two o'clock. Antonio, always impatient, had been pacing up and down the bridge for hours. Fernando had stayed close to the cruiser, trying to stay in the shade as much as possible. When Padilla informed him that the team would be arriving shortly, he walked out to the middle of the bridge to meet Antonio.

"About time," Antonio said, adjusting his sunglasses. The September sun was sinking quickly in the western sky.

They watched from a viewing area on the bridge as the team steered down the river. He noticed the heavy gauge wire fence attached to the railing intended to prevent jumpers. The fence made it difficult but not impossible to jump. Sections of the fence had been cut away by wire cutters or pushed out from the railing, leaving gaps large enough for a normal sized person to squeeze through. Every few yards there was a phone connected to a suicide prevention hotline. Everything possible had been done to prevent suicides, and yet here they were watching the Search and Rescue team approach the bridge from upriver.

The team consisted of two orange and black rafts that came bouncing down the river, careening from one rapid to the next. He counted three men on each raft, all wearing helmets and life jackets. They maneuvered among the rocks by using long poles and ropes to stay connected. As they approached the bridge they slowed to a near stop to begin their search.

The lead raft steered over against the riverbank. The men on board looped a rope around a large boulder on the bank to stabilize the raft. Then they tossed another rope to the men on the second raft, who let the rope out slowly as they moved downstream searching the river for any sign of Jimmy's body. They proceeded down the river in steps, using this same technique: one raft secured to the bank, the other raft moving slowly downstream while the men on board dredged the water with poles and hooks and their hands.

When the rafts disappeared under the bridge he followed Antonio across the road to the other side of the bridge. About a hundred feet down the river the search raft spotted something ahead, a black object partially submerged in the river. Two of the men tried to pull the object out of the water, while the third held the rope steady. Making their work more difficult, the raft bucked and bounced in the current. The two men finally got hold of the object and slowly pulled it out of the churning water. He could see their disappointment when it turned out to be a black garbage bag leaking garbage as they hoisted it out of the water. This scene repeated, one false alarm after another, as they made their way down the river.

By 5 p.m. the team had searched less than a mile of the river.

A depressing thought occurred to him: at this rate, it could take days to find Jimmy's body. Days of standing out here in the hot sun waiting. Once again he cursed Jimmy.

Finally Padilla, stationed in the command vehicle, came walking up to them on the bridge. "Sorry, guys...they're gonna have to quit for today. They have to get down to Pilar before it gets dark. That'll take them about an hour. The truck is waiting for them there. But don't worry, they'll be back tomorrow morning. We'll find him. It just takes some time."

"How many days are we talking about?" he asked.

Padilla shrugged. "Depends. Some we find the first day. Others take a week or so. Since the current is fairly strong right now, I think it might take a few days of dredging."

"Goddamn Jimmy!" Antonio cursed.

"They should be back here by ten o'clock tomorrow morning, maybe earlier if they get a good start."

"Okay, thanks," Fernando said as Padilla turned to walk back to the parking area at the end of the bridge.

They followed Padilla to their car and drove off toward Taos, neither of them speaking. He was hot and tired and dehydrated from too much sun and in no mood to talk about anything.

Finally Antonio asked, "Do you think we should call Ruby and tell her about the will Jimmy wrote?"

Fernando had to laugh at that. "Hah! Think it'll stand up in court? Scrawled on a brown paper bag...one of those paper bags package stores use for bottles of wine or hard liquor?"

"Oh, I bet old Raoul Garcia can make it stand up."

Fernando laughed again. "If, that is, Jimmy's dead."

"What do you mean?"

"Just that. I wonder if Jimmy's really dead. We saw the duffel bag, the one filled with tools he used at Abiquiu. But what about his clothes, his backpack? I know he packed some clothes back at his studio because I found hangers tossed on the bedroom floor."

"Yeah?" Antonio was interested now.

"Not only that, but where's the booze? Jimmy never travels anywhere without booze, lots of it," Fernando said.

Antonio paused a moment and then said, "Maybe he dropped them off at his ex-wife's house."

"Exactly. And maybe she followed him to the bridge and took him back home after he abandoned the Subaru. No, it wouldn't surprise me if they never found his body."

"Then what do you want to do tomorrow?" Antonio asked.

"I think we should go back to Arroyo Hondo and stake out the ex-wife's house. See if there's any sign of Jimmy there. Maybe I'm wrong, but I just have a feeling that Jimmy's not dead."

The sun had nearly set by the time they pulled into El Pueblo. Once inside they drank glasses of water and took turns showering. Within the hour they felt presentable enough to walk down the street to the Taos Inn for dinner. The food was passable and the Spanish classical guitar player even better. After a few drinks both of them were feeling better.

"So I guess we won't call Ruby about the will," Antonio said, feeling no pain.

"Not until we have an actual body. I'll believe it when I see it."

"You know, at first I thought you were crazy when you mentioned it, but I can see Jimmy faking his suicide," Antonio said. "He's a tricky little bastard."

"Yeah, especially when he has an accomplice to help him. Another ex-wife under his spell."

Antonio laughed. "The Jimmy spell."

On their way back to the motel they stopped at a tourist shop and bought straw hats for the next day's stakeout. Antonio went directly to their room while Fernando stopped at the office to extend their stay once again.

The same woman greeted him at the front desk. "Another night?"

"Yes please."

"Today I give you extra special multiple night rate," she said, writing the amount on a notepad and pushing it across the counter.

"Very generous," Fernando said.

"So how long you stay?

He laughed. "Who knows? I might be here forever."

She smiled. "The weekly rate is even cheaper."

At the thought of another week at El Pueblo he lost his sense of humor. He walked outside into the cool evening air, trying to clear his head from too many beers.

Walking to their room he saw an olive green van pull into the Kachina Lodge across the street. Looked familiar. Then he remembered.

He stopped and watched the van disappear into the huge Kachina parking lot. In the semi-darkness he couldn't tell for sure if it was the same van they'd seen yesterday. He went inside to tell Antonio. Coincidence?

25

Fernando awoke foggy from too many beers the night before. Big mistake. The bed creaked when he crawled out and stretched his hands above his head to see if he could actually feel all his limbs. He hobbled into the bathroom and swallowed two aspirin for his headache. Next he pulled the curtain closed on the window so he wouldn't have to watch Antonio jumping and flopping around outside in his exercise routine. Only then did he brew himself a cup of coffee and sit down in the one and only chair in their room to think. If Jimmy had faked his suicide, he must be in cahoots with Lauren, his ex-wife. She could help him with transportation and provide a place to stay for as long as he needed to hide out. Where better to hide out than a partly hidden farm in obscure Arroyo Hondo?

Later Antonio came bursting through the door with way too much energy. "Good run this morning. Five miles out to the Pueblo and around past the casino and back here."

"Please. I don't want to hear about it," Fernando said.

"And hey, I ran through the Kachina Lodge parking lot across the street. That is the same Ford Expedition we saw earlier."

After Antonio showered they walked down the street to Michael's Kitchen.

By the time they finished breakfast, ordered take-out sandwiches for lunch, and walked back to the room it was nearly nine o'clock. They packed up whatever supplies they would need for the day and then drove off on Paseo del Pueblo Norte heading for Arroyo Hondo.

On Rio Hondo Road Fernando drove by the turnoff to Lauren Mackey's farm and bounced over the dirt road to the river. He was relieved when he saw the empty parking lot by the trail to the hot springs. The last thing he wanted to see this morning was a group of young people frolicking in the nude. Antonio might decide to join them and toss off his uniform.

Fernando pulled behind the familiar outcropping of rock and locked the cruiser. With their sunhats and water, they walked around to their lookout from the day before. He found an old towel spread out on the ledge of rock and a couple of used condoms tossed in the sand. Evidently the young people last night did more than just soak. He didn't see a trash receptacle anywhere, so he ignored the towel and the condoms.

He found a comfortable spot leaning against the boulder and took out his binoculars. He surveyed the farm but found no sign of Jimmy or his ex-wife. No activity of any kind. Then he noticed that both vehicles they'd seen in the driveway the other day were gone. The Prius and the old Chevy pickup were nowhere to be seen. That puzzled him.

At noon they ate their sandwiches and washed them down with bottles of water. After they finished, Antonio asked, "What if the Search and Rescue team finds Jimmy's body today?"

The question hung in the air. Fernando hadn't thought of that. Another misstep. He checked his cell phone to see if they had service out here and found they didn't. What he feared.

"Good question. I'll have to call Padilla tonight when we get back to Taos. There's nothing we could do to help anyway," Fernando said.

That seemed to satisfy Antonio, who wandered off toward the river.

Sometime later Fernando saw the Prius come down the unmarked dirt road and pull into the driveway. The same woman as before climbed out of the car and carried two bags of what looked like groceries into the house. She made one more trip to the car and then slammed the door closed.

By this time Antonio was bored out of his mind. The big man couldn't stay still for very long. Every so often he hiked down to the river and over to the hot springs.

Clouds formed over the Taos mountains about three o'clock in the afternoon. Soon a front moved in from the west behind them, blocking the sun and bringing cooler temperatures.

As the day cooled the woman appeared in the garden with her basket. Again she walked down the narrow rows picking corn and tomatoes, chile and squash. When her basket was full, she carried it back to the house and placed it on a patio table. Then she disappeared in a small shed beside the patio, returning moments later wearing heavy gloves and carrying a hoe.

He watched her return to the garden and start weeding. She moved slowly, methodically down one row after another digging with the hoe. Every once in a while she stopped to rest and wipe sweat from her forehead.

She worked until dusk drained most of the light from the eastern sky. Then she went back to the house and took her basket inside.

Minutes later Fernando saw lights and then a dust cloud in the distance. A vehicle was approaching, slowly making its way down the dirt road. He waited, focusing the binoculars on the driveway. As soon as the old Chevy pickup came into view he suspected it was Jimmy driving.

The pickup swerved into the driveway and came to a stop behind the Prius. Out jumped Jimmy carrying a small bag. He looked around, as if checking to see if the coast was clear and then hurried to the front door of the house. He knocked loudly and disappeared into the house as soon as the door opened, shoving past his ex-wife Lauren.

"Antonio," he called out, not knowing where the big man had gone.

Antonio came running up from the river.

"Jimmy's here. He just arrived driving the pickup and went into the house," Fernando said.

"Good. Let's finish this so we can get the hell out of here."

Fernando raised his hand. "Okay. Slow down. We need a plan."

Antonio listened.

"I'll go around to the front of the house," Fernando said. "You go to the back door and knock. If no one answers, break down the goddamned door and go in hot. I'll be waiting for him out front by the pickup. Once he's in our custody you can hold him while I climb back up here and get the cruiser. Got it?"

Antonio nodded. "The little fucker won't get away this time."

They crept down the ridge to the first outbuilding and stopped to make sure they hadn't been seen. Nothing stirred, so they moved slowly up to the flagstone patio and paused. Again, nothing.

Antonio positioned himself beside the back door, while he crept around the side of the house, ducking below a small window. He hid between the Prius and the pickup and waited.

He didn't have to wait long. Before he could get out his service revolver he heard Antonio pounding on the rear door.

"Open up, Police!" Antonio shouted.

Suddenly all hell broke loose.

The front door slammed open and Jimmy came running out with

Lauren trying to hold him back screaming, "Come back inside! They'll kill you! Jimmy!"

Jimmy wrestled out of her grasp and took off running.

Fernando jumped out from behind the Prius and tripped Jimmy, who sprawled in the dirt cursing.

"Don't move! You're under arrest," Fernando said, leaning over Jimmy.

"Get offa me, Lopez, you fucking asshole. I didn't kill her."

"Then come with me and help me find the killer. I need your help."

"Yeah, like you're gonna help me, you and all the other cops," Jimmy said, raising to his knees.

Fernando jumped on top of Jimmy and wrestled him back down and reached for his cuffs when Lauren came running up and started hitting him over the head with a broom handle.

"Leave him alone!" she screamed.

The first blow grazed his ear but the second hurt like hell. Fernando turned and grabbed the broom handle and tried to twist it out of her hands, which allowed Jimmy to roll out of his grasp.

He lunged at Jimmy but missed and fell flat on his face in the gravel.

Instantly Jimmy was up and running down the driveway.

Just then he heard a car on the road out front. Out of the corner of his eye he saw a smudge of green, olive green.

"Thok thok! Thok! sounded from the road.

Jimmy collapsed in the driveway. Dark red blood bubbled out of his chest.

Lauren dropped her broom and rushed forward screaming. A small woman with glasses and a long gray ponytail, she ran over to Jimmy and cradled him in her arms. She tried to pick him up, to move him out of harm's way. Her face was sunburned to the color of brick.

"Call Nine One One! Call Nine One One!" Fernando kept repeating until she finally heard him and ran back into the house to call.

Antonio came running around the side of the house. "What's happened? Where's the shooter?"

"Stay with Jimmy!" Fernando shouted and ran toward the road.

Then he saw it. The Ford Expedition that had been following them. About forty yards down the road.

The oversized vehicle tried to turn around in the road but caught a wheel in the ditch. The tire spun in the loose sand and kicked up a cloud of dust and debris. Finally the tire caught and the van bounced onto the road.

Running toward the van Fernando pulled out his .41 Magnum and fired a shot that shattered the rear window.

Instantly a rifle poked through the busted glass.

Fernando dove into the ditch as the bullet zinged in the sand behind him.

He kept firing at the van as it sped away toward Rio Hondo Road and then disappeared.

With the van out of range, he picked himself up and walked back to the house. He saw Antonio leaning over Jimmy and pressing a bandana against his wound trying to stop the bleeding.

"Goddamnit! He's bleeding out," Antonio said. "If we weren't out in the fucking boondocks. Goddamnit!"

Ignoring Antonio, he bent over Jimmy. "Jimmy? Can you hear me? Who killed Kim?"

Jimmy opened his eyes momentarily. He tried to speak. "She... brought...with her...." And then he faded out. His eyes closed.

"He's gone," Antonio said, searching for a pulse.

A moment later Lauren rushed out of the house screaming at them. "Get away from him, you fucking pigs!" She shoved Fernando out of the way and then pulled Antonio off Jimmy.

She cradled Jimmy in her arms and wept. "You fucking bastards! You killed him. You killed my Jimmy."

He and Antonio looked at one other. They'd brought the killers right to Jimmy's door. They'd unwittingly participated in Jimmy's execution.

"He's dead. You killed him!" Lauren wailed.

26

They stayed with Jimmy until the ambulance came to take the body away. It was the least they could do for Jimmy and Lauren. Anyway, it would have taken too long for them to climb the hill to their car and then chase the Ford Expedition, so they'd stayed put. They didn't have a license number for the APB, which meant the odds of finding the vehicle were not good. Lauren had been hysterical until the EMTs treated her for shock. She insisted on going to Holy Cross Hospital in Taos with the body. One of the EMTs said he would bring her back home later.

So now they watched as the EMTs loaded the stretcher into the van. Lauren sat in the back of the van with Jimmy, holding his hand. Mute with grief, she gave them the finger when the EMTs closed the rear door. Seconds later the van drove off slowly, sadly, with its grim cargo. They watched the dust cloud traveling east on Rio Hondo Road.

Now, after all the mayhem, a wall of silence descended on them. Only the whisper of the wind bringing in a late September storm could be heard. Heavy clouds were moving in from the west, blocking out the last rays of the sun. Night had fallen.

"Well, shit!" Antonio said, kicking at the gravel in the driveway. "I feel like a goddamn fool."

"We didn't know," Fernando said.

Antonio shook his head. "Did you get a good look at them?"

"No. I think there were two, a shooter and the driver," Fernando said. "They were in that olive colored van. I'm sure it's the same van we saw at the river and then on the Plaza and at the Kachina Lodge. They followed us all the way from Santa Fe. That means someone sent a hit squad to kill Jimmy and we led them right to Jimmy without knowing it."

"I don't get it," Antonio said. "Who would send a hit squad to kill Jimmy?"

"Good question."

"What did Jimmy say to you? Right before he died?" Antonio asked.

"He said 'she...brought...with her.' I think he was trying to tell me Kim brought someone with her the night she was murdered. I don't know, maybe the murderer."

Antonio nodded. "That would make sense. It matches what Blaine told us at Ghost Ranch. That Kim had someone in the car with her."

"Yeah, except Rose said Kim was alone when she saw her drive by that night," Fernando pointed out.

Before leaving, they searched the house but found nothing of interest, just a tattered backpack stuffed with Jimmy's clothes and a couple of unopened bottles of vodka on the kitchen counter. Jimmy's stuff.

Fernando led the way, hiking up the gentle slope to the hot springs. They found two lowrider cars in the nearly dark parking lot and heard a group of young people frolicking in the hot springs.

Antonio chuckled. "Shall we take a look?"

He frowned.

"Suit yourself," Antonio said, disappearing down the trail to the hot springs. He came back a few minutes later with a big smile on his face. "Man, I've never seen so many tattoos in so many places. Positively distracting."

They climbed into the cruiser and eased out onto the dirt road, bouncing over the uneven terrain. Fernando drove slowly, carefully back to the highway and then pulled over at a rest area outside of Taos.

While Antonio watched, he stepped out of the car and called the station on his cell phone. He explained to the night desk clerk what had happened. Jimmy was dead, gunned down by two men in Arroyo Hondo. The desk clerk put him on hold and sent the call through to the Chief, who was still in his office.

"Good work, Fernando," the Chief said, obviously pleased by the news. "Now we can close the case and make everyone happy. The Mayor will be relieved that the murderer is dead. Justice for Kim."

"Well, wait a minute," Fernando said. "I don't think Jimmy is the murderer. We need to find out who killed Jimmy, and then we'll have a better idea of who killed Kim. Are you listening to me?"

The Chief did not respond.

"Jimmy's not a killer. He's a drunk who forgets more than he remembers, yes. But he's not a killer. Are you listening?"

Still the Chief did not respond.

"Especially women. Women love him, even his ex-wives."

"Fernando, listen...the Mayor wants closure. We have an arrest warrant out for Jimmy. We have Kim's blood on Jimmy's shirt. Now Jimmy's dead. It's a perfect end to the investigation."

"Yes, but I think he's innocent," Fernando said.

"That's only your opinion. No one here agrees with you. I want you to come back to Santa Fe and close the case, understand?"

Fernando ended the call before the Chief could continue.

He was beginning to understand, all right. The Mayor wanted Jimmy dead—and blamed for Kim's murder. Why?

Fernando climbed back into the cruiser and slammed the door.

Antonio looked puzzled. "Something wrong?"

Fernando waited until they were entering Taos to tell Antonio about his conversation with the Chief. "He wants us to drop the case."

Antonio stared at him. "Why? Doesn't he want to find out who killed Jimmy?"

"No, he wants the case closed. Now that Jimmy's dead, he can say justice has been done. Tit for fucking tat."

Antonio brooded. "Are you sure it's the Chief who wants this?"

"Good question. I suspect it's the Mayor who really wants it and the Chief is just going along to keep his job."

"And...?"

"And you can figure it out," Fernando said. "He's protecting someone...maybe himself."

"Christ. What are you going to do?"

"I'm going to find out who killed Jimmy. And Kim."

Antonio glanced at him. "Are you sure that's the wise thing to do?"

"What do I care? I'm retired, remember?"

27

Bad news travelled fast. Fernando had no more than walked into their house on Acequia Madre when their kitchen telephone rang. Estelle answered it and quickly pulled the receiver back from her ear. He could hear screaming coming from the other end of the line all the way across the room. Whoever was calling was not a happy camper. Well, what else was new?

"Here, it's for you," Estelle said and handed him the phone. She gave him the Evil Eye and walked out of the room.

Fernando sank down in a kitchen chair exhausted and dispirited from the long day. The last thing he wanted now was to listen to someone scream at him over the phone. He'd already been yelled at enough for one day.

He answered the phone expecting Lauren Mackey to be on the other end. "Lopez here."

"Fernando, you fucking pig, you killed Jimmy! You were supposed to protect him and instead you let them kill him. Why didn't you intervene? You could have saved him."

He tried to respond to the familiar voice and then gave up, listening to Ruby's tirade of profanity-laced accusations.

"He was in your custody, goddamnit! You were supposed to protect him. Instead you let them kill him right in front of you. An execution."

"Ruby...Ruby...listen to me," Fernando mumbled finally. "I didn't kill Jimmy. Some guys in a van drove by and shot him as he tried to run away. We haven't identified them yet, but we will. I promise you. It's just a matter of time."

"Hah! Why should I believe you? You stood there and let them kill him."

Ruby launched into another tirade about his empty promises and his failure to go after Kim's real killer instead of blaming it on Jimmy. "You haven't done a damned thing except target Jimmy. I've told you all along, he didn't kill Kim!" she shouted.

He listened until she ran out of gas. Then he asked, "How did you hear about Jimmy's shooting?"

"From Lauren, of course. She called from the hospital. You didn't even go to the hospital with her after you let them kill Jimmy. What kind of cop are you, Fernando?"

He sighed. "Okay, Ruby, I suppose you're right. Things haven't exactly turned out the way I'd intended. But you haven't been all that helpful either. Instead you've withheld information and sent us on wild goose chases. Maybe we could find Kim's killer if you would be more forthcoming. Instead of complaining, why don't you help us out?"

Silence.

"So let's talk...I want you to tell me everything you know about what happened that night at Jimmy's studio," Fernando pleaded. "Everything. The truth. I don't care who it implicates. Understand?"

She took her time responding. "I guess I could meet you at El Farol tomorrow afternoon. Say about four o'clock?"

"I'll be there. And Ruby...we will find Jimmy's killer, I give you my word."

She hung up on him without responding.

As soon as he hung up the phone Estelle appeared. "Dinner's in the refrigerator. I didn't know when you were coming home...or if you were coming home. Last night you didn't even bother to call."

"Sorry. I just never had a chance."

She turned her back and walked out of the room.

Fernando took his dinner out of the refrigerator and warmed it in the microwave. Then he sat at the table and picked at his food, brooding over the day's events.

He came up short no matter how he looked at his balance sheet. Two murders and both perpetrators still at large and likely to remain that way if the Chief and the Mayor had their way and closed the investigation. He should have stayed retired, quit when he was ahead.

Except he wasn't a quitter, never had been.

Tomorrow morning he would get back to work. Maybe Ruby would give him that one piece of information he needed to understand what happened at Jimmy's studio. To figure out who stuck the knife in Kim

Martin's chest and then placed her in the trunk of her car.

Then, too, he had to find out who killed Jimmy.

Meanwhile he would have to keep a low profile at the station, avoiding both the Chief and the Mayor, both of whom wanted him to close the case. What they really wanted was to get rid of him. But why?

Finished eating, Fernando washed his dishes and put them away, enjoying the mundane domestic chores that took his mind off the case and put some distance between him and his stressful day.

He took a long hot shower and then went to bed early, joining Estelle who already had her back turned away from him.

Welcome home.

28

Fernando slept late next morning. By the time he got out of bed Estelle had left the house. She and several other volunteers from the Saint Francis Immigrant Outreach Program were starting a massive food and clothing drive today, collecting food and clothing donated by grocery stores and businesses throughout the city. With winter coming on, their goal was to collect enough food and clothing to feed and clothe the approximately one hundred immigrant families in Santa Fe through December. Other groups of volunteers working through the church were soliciting doctors and lawyers for donations of medical and legal services. He respected Estelle's work for Saint Francis. Sometimes, though, he wished she respected his work as much as he respected hers.

After breakfast, he took a cup of coffee into his study and booted up his computer. He signed into the station's data systems and searched for any Ford Expeditions in the stolen car databank. He gave up after about an hour, finding nothing recent that seemed to fit his criteria. Later he called the Medical Examiner's office in Albuquerque to ask about Jimmy's autopsy. He was told the bullet that killed Jimmy pierced his heart and right lung. Looked like a 5.56 mm. round, fired from an automatic rifle.

After lunch he took a brisk walk along Acequia Madre, an exercise he'd started during his medical leave. The walk and the fresh alpine air invigorated him. Afterwards he sat on his patio soaking up the warm afternoon sun. When his cell phone rang he decided to ignore it until he saw Antonio's name.

"Fernando, it's Antonio. I think I may have just seen the Ford Expedition from Taos. I was driving down Lincoln Avenue to the post office and checked the rear view mirror before turning and there it was, parked on Lincoln. I had to go all the way around the long block to check it out, and by the time I got back on Lincoln it was gone. I'm pretty sure it was the same one."

"Did you get a license number?" Fernando asked.

"No, like I said, I just caught a glimpse of it in my rear view mirror."

"How far up Lincoln?"

"About halfway between the post office and city hall," Antonio said.

"No kidding? City hall. Interesting."

"I'm driving around the Paseo now looking for it."

"Okay. Let me know if you see it again," Fernando said.

He left for El Farol about 3:45 p.m., giving himself enough time to find parking. It might be late September, but there were still a few tourists in town cruising for local hotspots like El Farol.

He found a parking place in the lot across the street and walked over to El Farol. This time he saw Ruby sitting by herself at a corner table. She looked like she'd just come from her potter's wheel, with a red bandana tied around her head and flecks of clay on her shirt. She seemed embarrassed to see him, a first for Ruby in all the years he'd known her.

"Sorry about what I said last night. I'd been drinking," she said.

Fernando laughed. "I wish I had been drinking."

"I shouldn't blame you. It's just that the goddamn cops always go after the Jimmys of the world, the little guys," Ruby said.

"I hear you."

"The fix is in, Fernando. They're gonna put all this on Jimmy. Kim's murder, I mean."

Fernando nodded. "Looks like they're trying to, which is why I need your help. What did Jimmy tell you when he stopped by your place on his way out of town? Did he know who murdered Kim?"

Ruby shook her head. "He wouldn't say. All he said was that he'd helped put Kim's body in the trunk of her car. He used the first person plural: 'We' put her body in the trunk. He wouldn't say who that other person was. Out of a sense of loyalty, I suppose. I don't know."

"That explains how he got Kim's blood on his shirt."

When the server came over and asked what he'd like, Fernando pointed to Ruby's margarita. "I'll have what she's drinking."

Moments later the server brought his margarita. He raised his glass. "Cheers."

"Cheers to what?"

"Well, we know the person who helped Jimmy put the body in the trunk was one of the people who were there that night: maybe Blaine or Rose."

Ruby shook her head. "There you go again. You're forgetting the obvious: the fucking Mayor. He was a wife abuser, you know?"

Fernando nodded.

"And don't forget June Bryan, the half owner of Essentia," Ruby said. "The Bryan's have an open marriage. She and Jimmy got it on every once in a while. They were fuck buddies."

"Damn, isn't anyone monogamous anymore?" Fernando asked.

"Hah! Not on Canyon Road."

"How about Kim? Were she and June lovers?"

"I don't know about Kim and June," Ruby said. "All I know is that all the women loved Jimmy. They were all sleeping with him. Even when Jimmy and I were married they were all sleeping with him. The pig."

He laughed.

"What about you, Fernando? Have you always been monogamous?"

"Well...for the most part."

"Hah! There you have it."

They sipped their margaritas in silence for a few seconds, staring at each other.

Fernando broke the ice. "What else haven't you told me? Anything would help."

"Just that I knew Jimmy was going off to stay with Lauren. He told me he'd be there for a week or more because he knew the cops were trying to pin the murder on him. He was protecting someone...or maybe just afraid to name names. Kim ran with some powerful people."

Just then the door to El Farol flew open and in walked Blaine Rogers larger than life. "God-damn I need a drink. Pour me a shot of tequila and a beer chaser, darling," he said to Anne, the bartender.

Anne laughed. "What else is new? You always need a drink, Blaine."

Blaine looked around wildly and spotted them in back. "Ruby. Damn good to see you." He wore a khaki fishing vest over a white T-shirt and bright red Bermuda shorts.

Blaine walked quickly, like an overweight linebacker stalking his prey. His footsteps echoed on the wooden floor.

"Make room for one more," Blaine said, moving another small table up against theirs and sitting down heavily. "Fernando, how's it going, man?"

"What are you doing here?" Fernando asked.

"Yeah, aren't you supposed to be teaching a photography workshop at Ghost Ranch?" Ruby asked.

"Hah! I walked out on them. It's supposed to be a studio workshop, but these assholes didn't even know how to use a camera. Explain that to me. All the cameras are digital today, for fuck's sake. All you gotta do is point the camera and push the shutter release button. A fucking monkey could do it."

Ruby laughed. "I had the same experience the last time I taught a pottery workshop up there. It was like they'd never seen a pottery wheel before...or operated a kiln."

"Yeah, so I just walked out. I told them to find some other schmuck to teach the idiots, I didn't have time to waste on losers. Plus, when I heard the news about Jimmy, I knew I had to get back. I got lots of work to do at the gallery, man. I need to put up new signs and everything."

"Hey--wait a minute," Ruby said. "Jimmy left everything to me. That includes his paintings."

"Yeah, but you want me to sell them, right? I've sold all of Jimmy's work for more than fifteen years. I'll take my twenty percent. You still end up with eighty percent for doing nothing."

Ruby laughed.

Blaine held up both hands as if framing a photo. "Last Paintings of the Late Great Jimmy Mackey. I can see it now. When Tommy Macaroni died a few years back, the price of his paintings went up more than fifty percent. And let's face it, Jimmy was a hell of a lot better painter than Tommy. I gotta throw out all the crap Dave and Wayne have on the walls and make more room for Jimmy's paintings. The Chopped Nudes will sell like hotcakes. Even the damn landscapes will sell if I lower the price. Too bad the tourists are leaving town. They love the fucking landscapes."

Ruby stopped laughing. "Jesus, Blaine, that's crass. That's low. Jimmy's not even buried yet and you want to make money on his death."

"That's the name of the game, baby. Dead painters sell better, just like dead writers."

"You're a fucking asshole."

"I know," Blaine said, just as Anne brought his tequila and beer. He tossed down the shooter and sipped the beer. "Ahhh, that's better."

Fernando turned his chair to look directly at Blaine. "So Blaine...did you help Jimmy put Kim's body in her car trunk?"

"What? Wait...is that where you found her body? Shit!"

"Did you help Jimmy?"

"No. I told you I'd already left by the time Kim arrived. Remember?"

Fernando nodded. "You said you saw Kim drive by with another person in her car. The thing is, Rose said she saw Kim drive by alone in the car."

"Then she's lying. There was someone sitting in the passenger's seat."

"Who was it?"

"I don't know. I didn't get a good look at her."

"Her?" Fernando asked. "Then it was a female?"

Blaine looked confused. "Oh...I guess so, because the person was small."

"Could it have been June Byran?"

"From Essentia? I doubt it. What would she be doing riding around with Kim at night? She had a thing going on with Jimmy, but I don't remember ever seeing her with Kim."

Ruby shook her head. "God, the more we talk about our sexual entanglements, the seedier it all looks. I gotta stay away from Canyon Road."

Blaine stood up and waved his glass at Anne. "Another round, my dear."

Anne brought the drinks and chastised Blaine for his familiarity, only partly in jest, and the long day's afternoon proceeded gently into night.

29

Fernando woke up with a massive hangover for the first time in years. Fucking Blaine. Blaine drank as much or more than Jimmy, even though as a big man he could handle the booze much better. He reminded himself to stay away from El Farol.

He drank an extra cup of coffee to subdue his headache and then popped an extra strength Tylenol for good measure. That helped.

Today he wanted to check out one loose end: June Bryan. Maybe he'd missed something when he questioned her earlier. She claimed to have seen the group of drunken revelers as they walked up Canyon Road to Jimmy's studio. Maybe she also saw what happened at the end of the night when Kim was murdered and placed in the trunk of her car by Jimmy and someone else.

He waited until Essentia opened at ten o'clock and then drove up Canyon Road to the sex shop. Once in the parking lot he checked out Jimmy's studio first. Yellow caution tape blocked the front entrance. Otherwise the place looked the same as it did the last time he was here. Nothing in front looked disturbed. Not yet anyway, though he suspected Blaine would be coming over soon with a court order procured by his attorney, the one and only Raoul Garcia, allowing him to take possession of Jimmy's last paintings. Knowing Blaine, he probably had price tags ready.

He opened Essentia's red door and walked into its cloud of lavender incense. The heavy fragrance always made him cough. It was worse than a damned cigarette.

Paul stood behind the counter rearranging sex toys on the shelves along the wall. When he heard the door open, Paul turned around holding a large purple dildo in his hand. He waved the dildo at Fernando.

"Detective Lopez, welcome," he said, a small man wearing his usual khakis and black polo shirt. "Sorry to hear about Jimmy. I liked Jimmy, even though he could get crazy when he drank. He was a gifted painter. He didn't deserve to be shot down like that."

"No, he didn't," Fernando said.

"Do you think he killed Kim...like they're saying?"

"I don't, but I'm still looking for answers. I need to ask June a few more questions."

"She's in back doing her morning yoga. Do you want me to get her?"

"Don't bother," Fernando said. "I'll find her."

He'd spent enough time at Essentia to know where June practiced her yoga. He walked behind the counter and down the hallway to June's yoga room. He stopped at the entrance, watching her adolescent girl's body stretch and slither on the padded mat. The way she arched her back and pumped her pelvic area made it look like masturbation. Maybe that was the attraction of yoga: masturbation. The only attraction he saw in such gyrations.

When she curled her leg around her head, every muscle in his body ached just watching. No thanks.

Fernando cleared his throat to announce his presence.

Her head swiveled around like a bird's to look at him. She was so tiny she looked like a child.

"June, excuse me for interrupting your routine. I just need to ask you a few more questions."

She nodded and untangled her limbs one at a time. Then she assumed the Buddha position. "No problem. Glad to help."

"You've heard about Jimmy, I assume?" he asked.

"I did. I'm still in a state of shock, I liked Jimmy."

"So I hear," Fernando said. "Did Jimmy ask you to help him put Kim's body in the trunk of her car?"

"What? Are you serious?" June asked. "No. Look at me. I wouldn't be much help lifting Kim or anyone else. She was...well, voluptuous."

He nodded. "You said earlier that you heard the group coming up Canyon Road from El Farol. They were loud enough to wake you up. Right?"

"Yes."

"What about when they got to Jimmy's? Could you still hear them?" Fernando asked.

"For a while, yes," she said. "Jimmy and Blaine were arguing. Later they were much quieter."

"Did you see or hear them when they left? Or were you actually driving around with Kim and not in bed?"

"No!" June said, a flash of anger showing on her face. "I was in bed the whole time, until...well, when they quieted down I wondered what was going on. Not that I'm a Peeping Tom or anything, just curious. So I got out of bed again and looked out our bedroom window. I saw two people in the shadows. I didn't recognize either of them. I was surprised because they were whispering, when earlier they were making so much noise. Does that make any sense?"

"Where were they standing?" Fernando asked.

"Behind the car. Near the trunk."

"Are you sure you didn't recognize them?" he asked.

"I assume one of them had to be Jimmy. Who the other one was, I have no idea."

"Could the other one have been the Mayor?" he asked.

"Joe Martin? I...I don't think so. There were no other cars around, so I don't know how he could have magically appeared."

"You knew the Mayor was jealous because Kim was sleeping around, right?"

June nodded. "Everyone did."

"What about you?" Fernando asked. "Were you jealous of Kim because she was sleeping with Jimmy?"

She blushed. "No way! I'm not a possessive person. I think you know Paul and I have an open marriage."

Fernando stared at her, waiting to see if she cared to add anything else. She didn't.

"Okay, that's all I have for the moment. Sorry to bother you so early in the morning."

She stopped him, her anger under control now. "Do you have any idea who killed Jimmy? He could drive you crazy, but I can't imagine anyone wanting to kill him."

Fernando turned and walked away without responding, tired of hearing that everyone liked Jimmy. If everyone liked Jimmy, why was his body stuffed in a drawer down at the Medical Examiner's office in Albuquerque?

"Everything okay?" Paul asked as he walked around the counter to the front door.

Fernando stopped and turned to look at Paul. "What do you think?"

"Oh, I just meant…."

Fernando stepped outside and slammed the door behind him.

30

When Fernando stepped out of Essentia he happened to notice the yellow caution tape in the rear of Jimmy's studio had come loose. He saw it clearly from Essentia's side of the parking lot. So he walked behind the gallery to check out the disturbance. One end of the tape had been ripped off a utility pole and now hung on the ground. Apparently someone wanted to gain access to the rear entrance. He moved cautiously forward into the shadows to inspect the door, a heavy wooden door that showed no outward evidence of tampering. He tried the door but found it locked tight. Maybe whoever tampered with the tape had second thoughts about breaking and entering and walked away. Or maybe not.

He circled the building, inspecting each window large enough to provide a point of entry, but found no evidence of an attempted break-in. False alarm.

His cell phone rang just as he climbed into his car. "The fix is in," he heard Antonio say as soon as he answered the phone. The second time he'd heard that in the last twenty-four hours.

He closed the car door and said, "So I'm told. I heard the same thing from Ruby yesterday."

"I walked by the Chief's office this morning," Antonio continued. "The door was closed, but I could overhear him talking to the Mayor inside. They're going to put you back on medical leave pending retirement and hand the case over to Manny."

"Manny?"

"That's what they said. They want Manny to finish the paperwork and close the case."

"And forget about Jimmy's murder."

"Exactly. They plan to put that on the back burner and let it become another cold case. With no intention of getting back to it."

He knew this was coming so he wasn't exactly surprised, just pissed. Fucking Manny. Not yet forty years old with the bearing and emotional maturity of a teenager, always joking and wisecracking. Manny never seemed to take anything seriously, even his job. It was hard to imagine him having the balls to stand up to the Chief and the Mayor.

Antonio continued. "Yeah, Manny didn't want the case. He argued with the Chief, told him you were more qualified...but in the end he had to follow orders. So don't be too hard on him."

"I know. I'm not blaming him."

"In fact, Manny wants to arrange a meeting with you. Can you meet us at La Choza for lunch? We don't have to worry about the Mayor showing up there. Or the Chief for that matter."

Fernando laughed. "Not upscale enough. Not downtown enough."

"Exactly."

They agreed to meet at noon.

Fernando drove downtown and parked on Alameda Street several blocks from the station. He had an hour to kill before meeting Antonio and Manny for lunch, so he walked over to the Plaza and sat on one of the benches. Every once in a while he liked to sit on the Plaza and just think. Watch the pedestrians crisscross the Plaza from San Francisco to Palace and then back again. He felt centered when he came here. This was his place, his history. This was where he belonged.

He'd made many of his most important life decisions sitting here. To get married. To enter the Police Academy. To join the Santa Fe Police Department. And many others.

Behind him a cool northern breeze kicked up leaves on the Plaza. The leaves on the trees were turning yellow and red, burned by the cold night air. Having just passed its equinox, the sun had lost much of its strength. In the evenings he smelled piñon wood burning in the fireplaces along Acequia Madre. Before long the Sangre de Cristo Mountains north and east of town would be topped with bright white snow and the winter tourist season would begin with the annual influx of skiers.

A few minutes before noon he walked back to his car and followed the Paseo to Cerrillos Road. He parked behind La Choza next to Manny's Ford Mustang. He had to laugh. The Mustang was another sign of Manny's immaturity. He didn't see Antonio's Jeep. The big man must have ridden with Manny. Hard to believe a man Antonio's size could fit in a damned Mustang.

He walked inside the funky restaurant and spotted them

immediately. They huddled together at one of the back tables, surrounded by colorful Mexican rugs and musical instruments hanging on the walls. As he approached Manny threw up his hands in mock horror.

"Don't hit me, don't hit me," Manny joked.

Fernando laughed. "Hah! You'll get your beat-down from the Chief."

"Don't remind me. The fucker wants me to close the Martin case immediately before I even look at it. What the fuck am I supposed to do?"

"The fix is in," Antonio repeated.

Manny looked at him. "So what am I supposed to do? The bastards will fire me if I don't follow orders, but if I close the investigation now, how can I preserve some semblance of professional self-esteem? Tell me?"

Fernando shook his head. "Here's what I'm thinking. Why don't you stay away from the station for a couple of days. Call in and tell them you're working on another investigation. Make up something. That would buy me some time. I think I'm close to breaking the case, I just need a couple of days," he said, a slight exaggeration.

"Yeah, but you're supposed to be on medical leave pending retirement," Manny said.

"It's not official. Not until I sign the papers. That's why I'm staying away."

"Okay...then give me a rundown," Manny said. "I know nothing about the case except the main suspect, Jimmy Mackey, was himself just murdered. I need to know more about what I'm supposed to be working on."

So over lunch Fernando brought Manny up to speed on the two murders and everything the investigation had turned up so far. By the time he finished, over an hour later, the server was bringing coffee for the three of them.

Manny raised his hand. "If I understand you correctly, one of the people who came to the studio with Jimmy that night was not only the murderer but the person who helped Jimmy put the body in the trunk of Kim's car. That means the murderer must be either Blaine or Rose or possibly Ruby, even though she claims to have left earlier. Yes?"

Fernando nodded. "Or June Bryan, the co-owner of Essentia next door. Like everybody else on Canyon Road, she was having an affair with Jimmy and may have been jealous of other women."

"Oh, yes, Essentia, the finest selection of dildos in Santa Fe," Manny said, laughing. "I was just in there last week. Shopping."

Fernando and Antonio stared at Manny.

"Just fucking with you...but I've heard stories about the place. Who hasn't?"

Fernando frowned. "Anyway, that's where we are now."

"And what about the two guys in the van who killed Jimmy? You have no idea who they are? Or who they work for?"

"No idea," Fernando said. "We have an APB out, but so far nothing's come in."

"Well. Shit. You know I'm not a big fan of the Chief, but in this case it's the Mayor who made the call. He's been all over the Chief down at the station. What's his role in all this?"

"Good question," Fernando said. "He and Kim had marital problems and were going through a rocky divorce. And we have testimony from an employee in the Mayor's office who claims to have seen the Mayor strike Kim on the day she was murdered. That said, we don't think the Mayor was at Jimmy's studio Saturday night. Or at least we don't have a witness who can put him there."

Manny brooded over all this, sipping his coffee. "Okay, I'll disappear for a couple of days to buy you some time. I can't promise you more than that because the Chief will be calling day and night. He already is."

"No problem, that's all I'll need," Fernando said.

They finished their coffee and paid the check and then made their way outside to the parking lot.

Fernando grabbed Antonio's arm. "Let's go pay Blaine a visit. See how many of Jimmy's paintings he's managed to get his hands on."

Manny climbed into his Mustang. "Okay, gents. Keep me informed."

Fernando and Antonio watched the Mustang squeal out of the parking lot and turn sharply into traffic on Cerrillos Road.

Same old Manny.

31

With Antonio on board Fernando drove around the Paseo to Canyon Road and up to Blaine's gallery, Picasso and Company. Santa Feans liked to joke the gallery was more Company than Picasso, but Blaine seemed to think Jimmy's Chopped Nudes followed in Picasso's footsteps, so what the hell? Blaine hadn't wasted any time after Jimmy's death. Just as he promised, a huge banner hung over the front of the gallery: "THE LATE GREAT JIMMY MACKEY'S LAST PAINTINGS FOR SALE: EXCLUSIVE TO PICASSO AND CO."

Antonio scoffed at the sign. "Knowing Blaine, he probably started working on the damn sign before Jimmy's corpse was cold."

"Wouldn't surprise me."

They were about to enter the gallery when Fernando's cell phone rang. He saw it was Estelle and answered right away. "Yeah, what's up?"

"Fernando, I'm frightened. There's a van parked at the end of our driveway. The driver just keeps staring at the house and won't go away. I don't know if he's looking to rob the house or what."

"What color is the van?"

"It's kind of green. Olive green, I guess."

"Shit! Stay inside and lock the doors, Estelle. Whatever you do, don't go outside. I'm on my way."

"Let's go!" he shouted to Antonio, who seemed to understand.

"The van?"

"Yes. It's in our driveway," Fernando said. "They're trying to intimidate me."

"How would they know--"

Antonio never finished his sentence.

Fernando jumped into the car and hit the ignition, waiting for

Antonio. The big man was half in, half out, when he spun the car around in the parking lot and shot out onto Canyon Road. He raced up Canyon Road and slowed down just enough to make a sharp left turn onto Camino Escondido and then turned left again on East Alameda. From there it was a straight shot down to the Paseo and around to Acequia Madre. Sure enough, the van was parked at the end of his driveway. He could see it as soon as they rounded the first curve.

Antonio pointed to the van. "That's it, the Ford Expedition. They have some fucking nerve." He reached for his service revolver.

Fernando cursed. "Now I'm angry! Someone's going to pay for this."

"Look--they're leaving." Antonio pointed again.

He braked, then hit the gas when he saw the van back out of the driveway and speed away fast on Acequia Madre. He followed. The van turned left on Garcia Street and raced over to Canyon Road, nearly running over a couple of tourists crossing the intersection. The driver swerved, screeching, and then shot up Canyon Road past El Farol and past Jimmy's studio.

Fernando kept stopping for pedestrians, falling further behind. But then the van seemed to slow down and wait for them. Not a good sign.

Eventually Canyon Road dog-legged to the right becoming Upper Canyon Road, where both vehicles had to slow down because of rocks and potholes. He could see the National Forest closing in on all sides of the road as he followed the van to a narrow dirt driveway off to the left, no larger than a goat trail. He bounced over a cattle-guard at the entrance and found himself engulfed in a cloud of dust thrown up by the van.

He slowed to a crawl, allowing the dust to dissipate. Up ahead an abandoned farm came gradually into focus: a derelict adobe house with a flat roof and a For Sale sign out front. Off to the left stood a water tank and a maze of connected livestock pens. Off to the right a flat bed truck and no less than four junked automobiles cluttered the yard and ruined what would have been a pristine view of the national forest and the Sangre de Cristo Mountains.

The van slowly pulled up in front of the house. He followed cautiously.

"I don't like this," Antonio said. "We're being set up."

He knew Antonio was right. He thought about turning around but decided against it at the last moment. He had only two days to finish the investigation. Crunch time might as well come now.

Fernando stopped next to the water tank about twenty yards behind the van. He wanted room to maneuver, just in case.

Antonio unbuckled his seat belt and took out his service revolver.

Fernando switched off the ignition and unbuckled his belt. He reached for the door handle.

Suddenly he saw a flash of light coming from the roof of the house.

Thok! Thok!

Instantly their windshield exploded, showering them with glass. Fernando felt the shards sting his face and blur his vision. He turned to look at Antonio and saw nothing but red.

Antonio's left ear had been shredded and blood streamed down his face.

They jumped out on both sides of the car and hit the dirt at the same time. Fernando rolled over once and then came to rest against the water tank. Antonio lay flat in open ground with nothing to hide behind.

Fernando scrambled behind the water tank. He aimed his .41 Magnum and squeezed off two rounds at the shooter on the roof of the house. The shooter ducked behind an old swamp cooler, giving Antonio time to claw his way behind the Plymouth.

Out of danger for the moment, Fernando wiped the blood off his face with the back of his hand and then his shirtsleeve. The right side of his face stung like hell.

He watched Antonio take a kerchief from his rear pocket and tie it tightly around his neck. Then he pulled one side of the Kerchief up over the bleeding ear and hooked it behind the earlobe.

"Are you okay?"

"I'll kill the sonofabitch," Antonio said, not bothering to wipe the blood off his face.

Fernando eyed the layout of the farm. The water tank and the livestock pens offered some protection. All the protection he would need. "I'll circle around behind the van."

Antonio steadied his Glock, aiming at the swamp cooler.

Fernando scrambled around the water tank to the nearest livestock pen. The sniper fired one round that tore through a wooden fence post ahead of him. Then the sniper turned his attention to Antonio, firing several rounds that pinged against the side of the Plymouth.

Antonio blasted away at the sniper, who kept ducking behind the swamp cooler and then popping up to fire another round.

Fernando crept along the last of the livestock pens looking for the second man. The van driver seemed to have disappeared. Not good.

He could see the van clearly as he came around the corner of the wooden fence. The driver's side door was still open. He debated what to do next. From this angle he couldn't see the swamp cooler on the roof, which meant the sniper couldn't see him down below. The problem would be the van driver, wherever he was hiding.

He decided to take a chance and quickly stepped out from behind the fence.

Just as quickly the van driver popped up over the hood of the van and fired.

Fernando felt the air current of the bullet as he hit the dirt hard, firing one shot at the shooter as he fell. His bullet ricocheted off the front of the van.

For a long moment that seemed like an eternity all was quiet. Neither of them moved. Time froze.

Finally Fernando squeezed off another round at the van's windshield, hoping the flying glass would flush the shooter. A portion of the windshield shattered. The shooter cursed.

He fired again just as the van driver stood up to shoot.

He heard the soft thud of the bullet strike the shooter. The van driver screamed in pain and ducked down. The bullet had struck his arm or shoulder.

"Throw your gun down and come out with your hands up," Fernando shouted. "This is the Santa Fe Police."

"Fuck you!"

"Who sent you to kill Jimmy Mackey?"

"None of your business. You're a dead man!" the shooter shouted.

"So I've heard. Now throw your gun down and come out."

Cursing, the driver shot wildly over the hood of the van. Then his anger made him careless.

Fernando braced himself on the ground waiting for what was about to happen.

The driver moved around the front of the van holding his revolver in front of him, a short stocky man wearing a brown shirt and fatigues. Raging mad, he fired repeatedly as he stumbled forward.

Fernando fired one shot, striking the driver in the chest. He watched the heavy-set man fall to his knees and stare at him. Then the wounded man attempted to raise his gun, his arm moving up in slow motion.

Fernando squeezed off another round. This time the driver fell face down in the dirt.

Fernando moved cautiously over to the driver. Not finding a pulse, he took the man's wallet out of his back pocket and checked the name. Tom Spain. He looked for a cell phone but didn't find one.

When the adrenaline rush began to subside, he could hear Antonio shouting at him.

"Fernando? Are you okay?"

"I'm okay. Where's the sniper?"

He realized it had been several long minutes since he'd heard gunfire from the roof.

"I don't know," Antonio shouted. "I don't think he's on the roof. Seems to have disappeared."

Skeptical, he rose to his feet and cautiously moved back to get a view of the swamp cooler. Antonio was right. He saw no sign of the sniper.

Fernando quickly moved to the side of the house, taking cover. Had the sniper gone inside the house?

Fernando inched his way to the front door, revolver in hand. The door had been kicked in, leaving only part of its frame hanging on the jam. Inside, piles of trash and debris littered the rough cut plank floor. All the windows had been broken out and graffiti covered the walls of the kitchen and front room. The place stunk of mold and dead animals, enough to make him retch.

In the back bedroom he found the source of the odor: a dead raccoon partially devoured by another wild animal, probably a coyote. No sign of the sniper there or in the adjoining bathroom.

Retracing his steps, Fernando walked outside and saw Antonio approaching the house, holding the bandana tight against his ear. Blood covered his shirt and pants. Cuts and scratches from the flying glass had pockmarked his face.

"Shit! Do I look as bad as you do?" Fernando asked.

"No, I got the worst of it," Antonio said. "I was sitting closer to where the bullet hit the glass. I'll be okay. Let's finish this."

They walked behind the house, no longer bothering with caution. He knew Antonio, incensed, would never stop until the sniper had been killed or captured.

"There," Antonio said, pointing to a trail leading into the national forest.

Halfway to the foothills a lone figure in fatigues struggled up the first ridge carrying his heavy rifle.

The sniper looked back, saw them, and stumbled ahead.

32

They followed the sniper up the trail into the national forest, gaining ground as they climbed the foothills. The gunman, a heavy man carrying a heavy rife, struggled on the rocky trail that zig-zagged up a steep incline. Eventually he stopped, out of breath, and took a position behind a boulder looking down on them. When they saw him level his rifle, they ducked behind whatever cover they could find on the hill. Fernando crouched behind adjoining clumps of sagebrush and chamisa, while Antonio ducked behind an outcropping of rock off to the side of the trail.

"We need to get closer," Antonio said.

The sniper fired off a quick burst. The bullets ricocheted down the hillside behind them.

"Stay down."

"Where the hell does he think he's going?" Antonio asked. "There's nothing between here and the ski basin. That's a hell of a long walk."

"No, he's probably planning to lay low until nightfall and then double back down to Canyon Road," Fernando said.

While they talked the sniper moved away from the boulder and began walking up the trail again, heading for the tree-line. Soon he would be high enough to enter the thick ponderosa pines that would provide better cover. Beyond the ponderosa pines the mountain hillside changed to a mixture of ponderosa and colorful Aspen, their bright leaves glistening in the late afternoon sunshine.

If the sniper made it to the aspen, they would never find him before dark.

So they climbed faster, steadily gaining on the gunman. When he stopped behind a stand of trees, they stopped and took cover while he shot wildly down the hill toward them.

This stopping and starting continued for a good thirty minutes until the sniper reached the thick ponderosa pines halfway up the mountain. The gunman set up behind a large ponderosa and shot at them again. This time the bullets came closer, kicking up dirt in front of them and slamming into nearby trees.

"Fuck! We'll never catch him before dark, not at this rate," Antonio said. "I'm gonna have to leave you here. I'll run the rest of the way. You can climb at your own rate."

"At my own rate? You mean slow?"

"Whatever. I just need to get within fifty yards. I'll circle around behind him in the trees. He won't even know what hit him."

"Wait...we need him as a witness," Fernando said, but Antonio had already run off into the trees. The big man moved like a professional athlete, quick and agile in spite of his size.

Fernando squeezed off a shot at the sniper to get his attention while Antonio jogged through the trees, a shadow among shadows. A blur.

The sniper returned fire. This time the bullet was too close for comfort. It slammed into the tree he crouched behind.

Fernando backed down the hill and crouched behind a rocky ledge.

Farther up he watched Antonio gliding through the trees, circling around behind the gunman. It took only minutes for Antonio to close the gap. When he came within range Antonio slowed down, creeping ever closer through a particularly tall stand of ponderosa pines.

Finally Antonio came within easy range.

"Drop your gun! Now!" the big man shouted.

The sniper spun around and fired off a wild shot in the direction of Antonio.

"Drop it or I'll shoot!"

The sniper fired again, his fatal mistake.

Antonio raised his pistol to eye level and pulled the trigger. The bullet struck the gunman in the side of the head. He fell backwards onto the cushion of pine needles covering the ground.

Antonio moved cautiously through the trees to where the gunman lay. He lowered his gun when he saw the sniper wasn't moving. He kicked the fallen gunman and then bent down to check for a pulse. Satisfied, he walked out into a nearby clearing and waved that all was clear.

Fernando waved back and then climbed up to join Antonio. He arrived out of breath and unhappy with the shooting.

"He didn't give me any choice," Antonio said in his defense.

Fernando nodded, looking at the dark red blood pooling under the sniper's head. He leaned over and took the man's wallet out of his pocket. "Duane Jackson," Fernando said, looking through the man's credit cards and driver's license."The van driver's name was Tom Spain. Run them through the system when you get a chance."

Then Fernando rummaged through the man's pockets until he found his cell phone. "We don't want the Chief to get his hands on this. We'll need it as evidence."

Antonio looked around. How do we get the body down?"

"Call Linda and ask for the medevac. They can land it in the meadow out there."

While Antonio called for the chopper, he called forensics and asked them to send a unit out for the driver's body back at the farm.

"Chopper should be here in less than thirty minutes," Antonio said.

So they waited out in the meadow for the SFPD helicopter. When it appeared in the sky, Fernando waved his arms over his head to get the pilot's attention.

The pilot dipped to one side to acknowledge contact and circled twice before slowly setting down in the meadow. The blades of the copter churned up dead grass and pine needles in mini bursts that looked like dust devils.

The pilot cut the motor and a young officer named Jerry jumped out the side door and crouched below the blades of the chopper. He walked over to them. "What's the situation?"

"Over here," Fernando said. "There's another one down at the farm below that forensics will pick up. The two of them led us into an ambush at the farm. This one's the sniper. These are the same gunmen who killed Jimmy Mackey."

Jerry looked at him funny. "No kidding? I thought you were off the Mackey case?"

"I am. Come with me," Fernando said, leading him up to the sniper's body next to the ponderosa tree.

Antonio joined them, picking up the gunman's automatic rifle and holding it at arm's length. "Gun like this...useless in close quarters."

"Doesn't sound like he planned to be in close quarters," Jerry replied.

The pilot, who he didn't recognize, brought a body bag and looked at the corpse.

"Nice shot."

"Took me a while to get in range," Antonio said. "All I need is about fifty yards and he's a dead man."

"Yes, he is...."

"Okay," Fernando said. "The man's name is Duane Jackson, you'll find his wallet in his back pocket. Take him to the morgue. Antonio here can go with you to do the paperwork since I'm about to be put back on medical leave or retirement."

Both Jerry and the pilot glanced at him.

Fernando turned to Antonio. "Have them clean up your ear in the Emergency Room while you're at the hospital. Give me a call later."

"Will do."

"I'll go down and meet forensics," Fernando said. With that, he left the meadow and made his way back to the farm.

While he waited for forensics, he checked the dead van driver's pockets one more time in case he'd missed his cell phone. He found nothing but the wallet. So he walked over to the Ford Expedition and climbed inside. The driver's cell phone was on the dash, easy pickings. He deposited the phone in his shirt pocket and opened the glove compartment. Right there in plain sight laid a fat envelope stuffed with hundred dollar bills. When he peeked inside the envelope he saw a handwritten note consisting of three words: "Here's your down-payment." Careless, he thought to himself. Very careless.

Now Fernando began to feel more confident. He continued searching for more evidence, knowing what the federal prosecutor in Albuquerque would require. He sorted through the various papers, receipts, and miscellaneous trash on the floorboards, front and rear. Nothing there. So he looked under the front seats and retrieved more receipts and scraps of paper. One wadded up paper turned out to be a copy of an email from none other than Al Monroe, the Mayor's bodyguard, to Tom Spain at his business, Have Gun Will Travel: Rent a Security Guard. The letter offered Spain $50,000 to pursue and "eliminate" a murderer by the name of Jimmy Mackey, with $10,000 to be paid up front and the rest when the job was finished. It was signed by Al Monroe and sent from an email address that he recognized immediately: "santafenm.gov/mayor." Bingo.

He smiled, knowing he had what he needed. Suddenly out of the corner of his eye he noticed the forensics van coming up the dirt road to the farm in a cloud of dust. No time to waste. He hurried over to his Plymouth and opened the trunk. Then he took all the evidence, including both cell phones, and placed everything in a locked metal box he kept in his trunk just for situations like this. He had the only key to the box on his keychain.

A couple minutes later the forensics van arrived, followed by a squad car driven by Manny.

"The body's over by the house," he said to Miguel and Teresa as they climbed out of their van.

"I'm surprised to see you here, Fernando," Miguel said.

"So everybody says. I guess I've been ghosted. I think that's the term people use these days."

Manny joined them. "Ghosted. That's exactly the right term. Chief won't be happy to hear about your involvement in this."

"Antonio's doing the paperwork," Fernando replied. "I told him not to mention my involvement."

"Good, that might work," Manny said.

"Yeah, and if he finds out, so what?" Fernando asked. "I haven't signed the papers yet. Chief can go fuck himself."

Manny laughed. "My feeling exactly."

While they talked Miguel and Teresa walked over to the body and began their examination.

Manny looked around. "So these are the guys who killed Jimmy?"

He nodded. "One guy's over by the house. The other's up on the mountain. Actually, he's on his way to the morgue now. Chopper picked him up a few minutes ago."

"You know...the more I think about it, maybe this will make the Chief happy," Manny said. "We have a blank slate now. Kim's killer is dead. Jimmy's killers are dead. Case closed. What could be more convenient?"

Fernando shook his head. "The truth?"

Manny laughed. "Hah! That would be most inconvenient for everyone involved. Believe me."

33

Before leaving the farm Fernando cleaned out his Plymouth. The car was an eyesore now with a scattering of bullet holes in its front end and a smoking engine leaking oil, water, and other vital fluids. Not to mention a missing windshield. Dead and gone. He took everything out of the glove compartment and grabbed the metal box in the trunk and moved it all to Manny's cruiser. Manny gave him a ride, dropping him off at his house on the way to Christus Saint Vincent Hospital to pick up Antonio in the emergency room. On the way they formulated a game plan. Manny would deal with the Chief and run a check on Jimmy's killers, while he laid low for the moment.

Fernando watched Manny drive off down Acequia Madre and then went inside their house to check on Estelle. He needn't have worried because she had already moved on from her encounter with the van. He found a note she'd left on the kitchen table: "Went to work at the church. Back at 6 or 6:30 p.m. for dinner. Estelle."

Over the years Estelle had become more religious, having worked for the parish in a number of jobs, most of them as a volunteer. Unlike Estelle, he had grown more skeptical about religion. Thirty-some years of police work had disabused him of a belief in divine providence. He believed in a material world, pure and simple. Occasionally he went to mass on Easter Sunday or Christmas Eve with Estelle and their two daughters but only to keep the peace and please Estelle. He figured it was the least he could do.

With Estelle gone he had time to research Duane Jackson and Tom Spain. So he fired up the Keurig and made himself a cup of coffee and carried it into his study. It took only minutes on his computer to discover that Jimmy's killers co-owned the private security company referenced in Al Monroe's email--Have Gun Will Travel: Rent a Security Guard. They specialized in one-time and temporary jobs, where one or both of them would work security. Their office was located in a strip mall out in Española, about twenty miles north of Santa Fe.

His cell phone rang while he was browsing their website.

"Fernando, it's Manny. Jackson and Spain own a private security company in Española."

"Yeah, I'm looking at their website now. What else did you find? Do they have criminal records?"

"No, they're clean," Antonio said. "I checked to see if Al Monroe had ever worked with them but didn't find any record of that. Still, it stands to reason they would know each other, working in the same field and all. I'll keep looking."

"Okay, thanks. Have you talked to the Chief yet?" Fernando asked.

"No, he's out of the office this afternoon. We're good so far. I'm leaving now and don't plan on coming back to the station tomorrow. Will that give you enough time?"

"I hope."

Fernando shut down his computer and brooded on this latest information. Jackson and Spain were guns for hire. Someone had hired them to kill Jimmy. He went over his list of suspects looking for someone who had a motive to kill Jimmy. He kept coming back to the Mayor. But something was missing, some key connection that would link the Mayor to what happened that night at Jimmy's studio.

While he brooded, the doorbell rang. Now what? A horrific vision flashed through his mind: the Chief standing outside with retirement papers in hand wanting him to sign on the dotted line.

Instead, when he opened the door he found Linda Aragon from the Mayor's office standing on his front porch. Her friendly face comforted him.

"Fernando, I'm so sorry to bother you at home," she said. The middle-aged woman with short hair and dark glasses was dressed in a running suit today.

"No, not at all. Come in."

He stepped back to make way for her. She entered timidly. He led her into the living room. "Can I get you some coffee or tea?"

"Oh, no, I don't want to trouble you. I just...well, I didn't tell you everything I should have when we talked."

"Okay."

"I was terminated, you know," Linda said. "From my job at the Mayor's office. Yeah, he said it was because I made too many mistakes, but I suspect it was because I talked to the police about what happened between him and Kim."

He shook his head, knowing he was responsible. "I can help. I'll talk to him and try—"

"No, it's okay. I'm going to take early retirement and get my city pension. I'll be fine. I was thinking about retiring anyway. It's just not much fun down there these days. Too much stress."

"I'm really sorry," Fernando said.

She nodded. "What I didn't tell you earlier is that Joe had been spending a lot of time with Rose. Even now she comes in every day to see him. They close the door, but I can hear them."

"You mean Rose Lucero, the Arts Critic at the *Independent*?" Fernando asked.

"Yes, she was part of the reason he and Kim were having marital problems," Linda said. "He was having an affair with Rose. That's really what their fight was about, when he slapped her."

"Really. I thought they had an open marriage. Why would Kim object if she were having relations with Jimmy Mackey and other people? At least that's what I've been told."

"Well, I think some of the gossip about Kim might be exaggerated, although from what I heard them say she was the one who brought Rose to him."

"What do you mean?" Fernando asked.

She blushed. "Kim and Joe were having sexual problems, so Kim arranged a threesome with Rose. You know, to excite him with a younger woman. Then Rose and Joe hit it off and Kim was left out. That's what I think happened."

"So there was friction between Kim and Rose."

"Yes, but Kim didn't like to show it. She did her best to control her feelings," Linda said.

"And Rose?"

Linda shook her head sadly. "She's a hard one to figure out. She's much too young to be involved with the Mayor. I think she's just been experimenting with the Martins and that Canyon Road crowd."

He laughed. "And they've been more than willing to experiment with her, I hear."

"Especially Ruby. She's another wild one."

"But what about Rose? Could she have been jealous enough to

murder Kim?" Fernando asked.

"I doubt that. She's too shy. Too proper. I can't imagine her being that violent. Ruby and those people on Canyon Road, maybe. But not little Rose."

"What about the Mayor?"

She shook her head. "Oh, I don't think...."

"You know he can be violent. You were in the office when he hit his wife. And you saw her running out crying and holding her face."

"Yes, but he just seems...I don't know, too careful, too calculating to do something that drastic."

"You'd be surprised what people are capable of doing. Especially when passions are involved," Fernando said, noticing that she was reaching for her purse.

Then he saw why. Tears were streaming down her face.

Fernando apologized. "I'm sorry if I upset you."

"No, I'm fine. It's just that I had such high hopes for the Mayor. And I really liked Kim. She was something special."

"So everyone says."

34

Over dinner Fernando told Estelle he'd decided to retire as soon as he finished this last case. He didn't explain why. He didn't mention the Chief and the Mayor wanting to get rid of him. He didn't mention what had transpired with the two shooters in the van who had frightened her. Some things Estelle was better off not knowing, even if she suspected he was withholding something horrific he didn't want her to know. Another close call.

Earlier she'd asked, "Where's the Plymouth?"

He'd mumbled something about a blown engine and the car having to be taken to the junkyard. RIP.

She'd eyed him dubiously but didn't comment.

Now her face brightened into a big smile. "Oh, thank God. Those guys in the van scared the life out of me. You have no idea what it's been like for me. For over thirty years I've watched you walk out the door every morning not knowing if you'd ever come back. That could have been you instead of Jimmy up in Taos. They could have killed you."

"Well, you won't have to worry any more," Fernando said. "This will be my last week. The Chief is working on the paperwork now."

After the dishes were washed and put away, they went outside on the back patio to talk and drink their habitual after dinner tea. Estelle wanted to discuss all the places they could visit once he retired starting with her favorite beach in San Diego, Coronado Beach. Maybe they could rent a house on the beach and their two daughters and their families could join them, she said.

Maybe, but at the moment he just wanted to relax and enjoy the view in their back yard. Estelle's rose bushes bordered the flagstone patio, with her purple larkspur and yellow black-eyed susans along the edge of their property. The leaves of the cottonwoods along the acequia were turning, the air fresh with the scent of pine. Their patio always cheered him, even after a long brutal day. The enclosed patio offered respite from a troubled world.

Estelle went to bed around ten o'clock. That gave him the opportunity he'd been waiting for. He walked around to their garage and climbed into Estelle's Camry, which he rarely drove. He didn't have any other choice tonight since the Plymouth had finally given up the ghost. He backed the Camry out of the garage and then eased out onto Acequia Madre. Once on the Paseo he followed it around to Don Gaspar and turned left. He found the house rented by Rose Lucero several blocks up Don Gaspar near a small park.

He slowed down to take a look. A porch light illuminated the front of the sweet little adobe, bordered on either side by tall sunflowers and hollyhocks. The light also reflected off two cars parked in the narrow driveway. Just what he hoped to find. He pulled into the driveway and parked behind the second car, a sleek black Mercedes. After what Linda Aragon told him, it didn't take much imagination to guess who owned the car. He switched off the Camry and listened through his open window. Not a sound anywhere.

He stepped quietly out of his car and paused a moment, letting his eyes adjust to the semi-darkness. A faint light glowed in the rear of the house even though the front rooms were dark. He moved stealthily around the parked cars, hoping the house didn't have a motion-detecting security system. Stepping up on the concrete porch he rang the doorbell once, waited a few seconds, and then rang it repeatedly. He stood back from the door when he heard shuffling noises inside. Someone was coming. Whoever it was wouldn't be happy to see him. They never were.

The lock clicked and then the door opened slowly, revealing the young face of Rose Lucero, her face half in shadow and half in light. She seemed stunned to find him at her door.

"Detective Lopez...what are you doing here?" she asked, opening the door wider.

He looked at the young woman, wearing a tight silk robe wrapped around her naked body. Barefoot.

"It seems I need to ask you some questions about your relationship with the Mayor," Fernando said.

Now he could hear rustling sounds coming from the rear of the house, as if someone was trying to get dressed in a big hurry.

She pulled the robe tighter around her. "Now? At this hour?"

"Why not? You busy with something else?" Fernando asked.

She continued to stare at him.

"Can I come in?" He moved toward the door.

"No! Not now. You can't come in without a search warrant."

"Sure, I can get a search warrant and come back," Fernando said. "Or I can have you brought in for questioning tomorrow morning. Which would you prefer?"

"I mean...why do you want to know about my private life? My relationships are my business. They have nothing to do with Kim's murder, if that's what you're implying."

"That's the question," Fernando said. "You and Kim were in competition for the Mayor's bed, right? And then she was murdered. You see the problem."

Rose shook her head. "I thought the investigation was finished. I thought Jimmy killed Kim."

"No, it's not finished. Not as far as I'm concerned," Fernando said.

"I don't like this...."

Then I would advise you to get a lawyer."

"I already have one," Rose said. "He's representing all three of us: Ruby, Blaine, and me."

"Raoul Garcia, no doubt."

She nodded.

"Okay. We'll talk at the station."

Fernando turned away and then paused for a moment. "Say hello to the Mayor for me."

Then he walked away, leaving Rose standing at the door with a pained expression on her face.

Fernando heard a man's voice inside as he opened the door of the Camry.

35

Linda stopped him as he walked into the station next morning. "Hey, Fernando, everyone's asking for you today. Chief wants to talk to you first thing. And you have a visitor. He's waiting in your office."

"Tell the Chief to get the papers ready," Fernando said. "I'll sign them at the end of the week."

She gave him a funny look.

"He'll know what I'm talking about. So who's in my office?"

Linda frowned and lowered her head. "I don't want to ruin your day so early in the morning."

"Never mind, I can guess," he said, walking down the hall to his office. Rose had warned him last night; he just didn't expect a visit this soon. He tried to put on his game face, wishing he'd taken the time to drink one more cup of coffee before leaving the house. Then again there was just no way to adequately prepare for Raoul Garcia. No way in hell.

"Lopez!" Raoul shouted as he stepped into his office. "Where you been, bro? I've been sitting here for fifteen fucking minutes. I got to be in court in less than an hour."

"Sorry to keep you waiting, Raoul," Fernando said.

"Hah! I can imagine."

"Long time no see."

"Yeah. It's been a while." Raoul reached over a pudgy hand studded with huge rings and shook his hand. He was dressed for court, wearing a light blue suit with a purple paisley necktie that glowed like neon. Just looking at the tie was a psychedelic experience.

"So what fire-bombing revolutionary are you defending this morning, Raoul?"

"Are you talking about the client I'm defending in court or the woman you harassed last night?"

Fernando shook his head. Same old Raoul. His curly black hair might be tinged with gray and his jowls might sag a bit, but Raoul was still larger than life. Relentless as a pit bull.

Fernando took a seat at his desk and sat back in the creaking wooden chair staring at Raoul, waiting.

"Jesus, won't they give you a decent chair?" Raoul asked. "The meth heads I defend have better furniture than this. You're getting the short end of the stick, my friend. You ever want to file an age discrimination or equal pay lawsuit, you know who to call."

"Thanks. I'll keep that in mind," Fernando said.

"Don't wait too long. My docket is full. With all the dopers and the cartels and the race wars, I can't keep up. Every motherfucker on the street is armed to the teeth and trigger-happy. They shoot each other and then come to Raoul expecting me to get them off with some lame-ass defense. Stand your ground, kiss my ass, or whatever."

Fernando laughed. "They're all guilty, you know."

"No shit!"

"So Raoul, how can I help you? Or need I ask?"

"You know why I'm here, Lopez. I got a call from Rose Lucero last night right after you harassed her. Don't deny it, you threatened and tried to intimidate her just because she happens to be young and stupid and fucking the Mayor. So what? Is there a law against fucking the Mayor that I'm not aware of?"

"He's married," Fernando said.

"Hah! So what?" Raoul asked. "That's not a legal issue, it's a matter of taste. Anyone dumb enough to fuck that asshole deserves pity, not harassment. You understand what I'm saying?"

Fernando sighed. "She said you were representing her...and Ruby and Blaine too. Is that right?"

"Sure, all three of them came running to me right away. They knew you would try to pin Kim Martin's murder on one of them."

"Come on, Raoul, you know me better than that."

"Yeah, I know you're an honest cop--if that's not an oxymoron. You're the only one down here I trust. Still, you take orders just like the rest of them. I wouldn't trust the Chief or the Mayor for one second."

Fernando nodded. "I hear you."

"So what happened to Jimmy as the prime suspect? It was his house and his knife that killed Kim, remember?"

Fernando shook his head. "I don't think he killed Kim."

Raoul frowned. "Well, you don't have one fucking shred of evidence, physical or otherwise, on anyone else. The only physical evidence you have is Jimmy's blood-stained shirt. You might not like it, but Jimmy is the only case you have."

"Maybe."

"Listen, Fernando, even if you could convince the District Attorney to charge any of these people, which you can't, the judge would dismiss it with a summary judgment. You have no case, nothing."

"Maybe," Fernando repeated.

"You surprise me. I thought you might go after Ruby or Blaine. If any of the three had the makings of a murderer if would be that crazy bastard Blaine. If not Blaine, then Ruby. But Rose? Sweet little Rose? Never."

"Yeah, but here's the thing, Raoul. Both Rose and Kim had been sharing the Mayor's bed. Sometimes together."

"Come on. Kim and the Mayor had been separated for months," Raoul said. "Rose wasn't jealous of Kim."

"Who are you trying to cover for, Rose or the Mayor?"

Raoul looked away. He shook his head sadly. "I hate the Mayor. He's a prick. But sometimes you have to cut your losses, man. You can only do what's possible. You take what you can get. Do you understand what I'm trying to tell you?"

He stared at Raoul.

"Use your political instincts, Fernando. I'm being serious now. Take what you can get. I'm telling you this as a friend."

"I hear you. Look the other way. Ignore the fix. Don't make waves. Is that right?"

"Listen, you have Jimmy all tied up in a ribbon and handed to you on a silver platter. Close the damn case and move on. Live to fight another day when you have a better hand."

Fernando stood up from the desk and walked around the office, stopping in front of the window overlooking Washington Avenue. From the window he could see the nearly empty Plaza.

Fernando couldn't let it go. The funny thing about it was that he disliked Jimmy, always had since the day Jimmy shot off part of his finger.

Fernando turned to face Raoul. "What about justice? Does that even mean anything anymore?"

"Jesus, Fernando. How long have you been in the criminal justice system? How many times have you seen justice?"

Fernando had heard this before from more people than he cared to remember. "You may be right, but you still have to try. You do what you can."

"That's what I'm saying, Fernando. Do what you can--do what's possible. And learn when to back off. What's the line from Shakespeare: 'Though justice be thy plea consider this, that in the course of justice none of us should see salvation.' I have the line framed and hanging on my office wall, along with my collection of Spanish wood carvings and Navajo rugs."

"Didn't know you were a Shakespeare fan, Raoul."

"Hah! There's more crime and murder and butchery in Shakespeare than all the law books on my shelves."

Fernando shook his head. "Let's get back to Rose. What's she hiding?"

"She's fucking the Mayor. She's embarrassed. You forget, she's only twenty-three years old. A child."

"Yeah, but there's something more," Fernando said. "I could tell by her reaction when I asked to question her."

Raoul sighed and shook his heavy jowls. "You're wasting your time, my friend," he said sadly. He stood up, a heavy man with a big belly, and walked out of the office without looking back.

36

Raoul's visit left Fernando in a sour mood. He respected, even admired Raoul, but something about the man always pissed him off. Maybe because Raoul was always right and always knew he was right. Though cynical as hell, Raoul's political acumen was as sharp as a razor. No one understood the politics of the New Mexico criminal justice system better than Raoul. A loudmouth Chicano from the barrio didn't get to his illustrious heights without being ten steps ahead of the increasingly Anglo establishment.

As a distraction he decided to go next door to the Great Burrito Company for another cup of coffee. On his way back into the station he found Antonio talking to Linda. The big man wore a padded white bandage covering his left ear. The thick bandage made his face look lopsided as though he had some sort of growth or goiter removed from the side of his head.

He glanced at Linda. The two of them burst out laughing.

"What are you guys laughing at?" Antonio asked, irritated.

"Sorry, Antonio," Linda said, "but you look like you've had one ear amputated."

"No, it just looks like you're on headphones, like all the young people," Fernando said. "Or in your case, headphone."

"Thanks a lot."

Fernando gave Antonio a pat on the back. "I'm going to be out of the office this morning, but I plan to pay the Mayor a visit this afternoon. Can you come along? Say about 1 p.m."

"Sure, I'll keep Al company while you have a heart to heart with the Mayor."

"Exactly."

Fernando saluted the two of them and retreated to his office. No more delays. It was closing time.

He checked his notes while drinking his coffee. To refresh his memory he reread Jimmy's last words: "She...brought...with her." He thought he understood what Jimmy was trying to communicate.

He finished his coffee and left the station again, walking up Marcy Street to the office of the *Independent*. Inside the receptionist nodded as he stepped through the door. "Can I help you?" she asked, a tiny woman with mousy brown hair and thick glasses. She waited for his response.

Fernando looked around the newsroom, where assorted reporters and copy editors sat at their terminals typing on their keyboards. "Yeah, I'm here to see Rose Lucero."

She paused, looking up at him. "She's not here. She resigned this morning. Said she was moving back to the Midwest."

"What?" He thought maybe he hadn't heard her correctly.

"I said she no longer works here. She quit."

The news took him by surprise.

Fernando nodded, looked around once again to make sure she wasn't there, and then exited the building. He walked quickly down Marcy Street to Washington and around to the station.

Instead of going inside he climbed into Estelle's Camry and retraced last night's steps to Don Gaspar. This time he found only a Passat station wagon in Rose Lucero's driveway. He parked behind the VW and walked up to the porch. The front door was open. Through the screen door he spotted boxes and suitcases stacked on the floor inside the front room. It looked like Rose was attempting to leave town fast before he could haul her down to the station for questioning.

He could hear her packing boxes in the rear of the house, oblivious to his presence.

He knocked softly and then stepped inside, moving cautiously around the boxes and piles of clothing. "Hello?"

Her head poked around the door to her bedroom. A look of dread flashed on her face. She froze.

"I see you're moving," Fernando said. "That was quick. And you resigned your position at the *Independent*."

She dropped the armful of clothing she held in her hands and stepped into the front room. She wore jeans and a white T-shirt and looked very, very young. Like a teenager.

"Yes, I have to get away from this place," Rose said, wiping the sweat from her forehead with her arm. "It's messing with my head. I need to get back to my college friends in Michigan. I'm not ready for this...."

Fernando nodded.

"Please leave me alone. I just want to leave and get back to my life and forget I ever came here."

""First, why don't you tell me what really happened the night Kim was murdered," Fernando said.

"I told you, I don't know who murdered Kim." She sounded desperate, on the verge of tears.

"Then let me tell you what I think happened," Fernando said, suddenly feeling as though he were speaking to one of his daughters. "You said you left Jimmy's studio early and were walking back home when you saw Kim on her way to Jimmy's. You said she was alone in her car, which was true until she stopped to pick you up. We know that because Blaine saw two people in the car as it came up Canyon Road. And because Jimmy's last words were something to the effect that Kim brought you with her."

She nodded, now wiping her eyes with the sleeve of her T-shirt.

"You and Kim started to argue when the two of you arrived at Jimmy's," Fernando continued. "You went into the house and came back with a steak knife. Then your argument with Kim turned violent and you stabbed her. You decided to put her body in the trunk of her car, but you couldn't lift her by yourself, so you went to get Jimmy to help you. That's how Kim's blood came to be on Jimmy's shirt."

She shook her head and burst into tears. "No! That's not what happened," she sobbed.

"Then tell me what happened, Rose. The truth."

She tried to compose herself. It took a couple of minutes for her to stop sobbing. He waited patiently, tempted to give her a hug as he would to Flavia, his daughter that most resembled Rose.

"Okay," she said finally. "It's true that Kim saw me walking home and picked me up. She was really drunk. She ran into the stop sign at the Garcia intersection. You can check the right front fender of her car and see the damage. By the time we got to Jimmy's she could barely get out of the car. She started calling me a little bitch, a little piece of fluff for her husband, saying he couldn't satisfy a real woman like her. Then she staggered up to the studio and started yelling at Jimmy. He was just as drunk as she was and started yelling back.

"When she came down to the car she had a knife in her hand. She waved it at me as if trying to scare me off. At first I thought she was just fooling around, but then she got this funny look on her face and tried to stab me in the stomach. I grabbed her arm and pushed back. We struggled and suddenly she seemed to go limp and the knife plunged into her breast. I was horrified. I jumped back and screamed for Jimmy to come help. Kim just looked down at the knife sticking out of her chest. She didn't speak. Not a word. In fact, she smiled. I think she thought it was just a silly accident that would go away if she waited long enough."

Rose shook her head, remembering. "That's when I saw the blood. The red spot on her shirt just kept growing. I reached out to help her but she swatted away my hand. Then she turned and staggered over to her car and climbed into the driver's seat. She just sat there staring at the knife and the bloodstain."

Rose shook her head. "I panicked. I screamed and ran up to the studio to get Jimmy. He was slumped over on the sofa, half asleep. I shook him awake and asked him to call Nine One One but he refused. Instead, he came down to look for himself. I felt a weak pulse, but Jimmy said she was already dead, good riddance to the bitch, something like that. So he opened the trunk and grabbed her under the arms and lifted her out of the car. He asked me to grab her legs, which I did, and then we placed her in the trunk and closed the lid. Afterwards Jimmy went back to his studio as if nothing had happened. I started walking home and then panicked. I ran the whole way. I was horrified. That's what happened. I swear to God. Please believe me."

"Who wiped the fingerprints off the knife?" Fernando asked.

"Jimmy did, right before closing the trunk."

"So Kim was still alive when you placed her in the trunk. She might be alive today if the two of you had called Nine One One."

Rose burst into tears. "I just wasn't thinking. It happened so fast. And they were both so drunk. I hate this place. I want to go home."

Fernando sighed. "What was the Mayor's role in all this?"

"Nothing. He wasn't there that night," Rose said.

"But afterwards, when he sent the two thugs to kill Jimmy?"

"Not to kill him...to find Jimmy and make sure he was arrested. He was just trying to protect me."

"Yeah, but they did kill Jimmy, and they tried to kill me," Fernando said.

"I don't know anything about that," she pleaded, wiping the tears that now streamed down her face. "Everything he did was to protect me. He's not a bad man, you know. He and Kim were just incompatible. He's cool and analytical, she's all passion and sexuality. I've never met anyone like her. Their marriage was a total disaster."

"If what you say is true...then Kim's death was an accident," he said, choosing his words carefully. "Not only that, but an accident she caused--by her intoxication. So why didn't you go to the police?"

"I just panicked," Rose said. "I was all by myself. Jimmy was too drunk to verify my story or remember what happened. I didn't think anyone would believe me."

Fernando took a seat on a nearby sofa and looked at her. They remained silent for several minutes, just looking at each other across the room. She'd stopped crying now, but her hands were still shaking.

"So when are you planning on leaving?" he asked finally.

"Just as soon as I get my stuff in the car," she said. "I don't have any furniture, so everything will fit. I plan to drive to Denver tonight. I have friends there I can stay with, and then I'll drive straight through to Michigan tomorrow."

"That's a long drive." He didn't know what else to say.

"It is, but I did it on the way here. I guess I can do it again."

Fernando nodded. "Okay, then. Have a safe trip," he said, getting up and heading for the front door.

"Detective Lopez?" she said, stopping him.

He turned around.

"Thank you."

37

Fernando sat at his desk staring into empty space. Finally he made his decision. He knew what he had to do. First, though, he took the emergency pack of Camel Lights out of his desk drawer and lit one. Fuck it, one cigarette wouldn't kill him. While he smoked he called Manny and told him to close the Kim Martin case. Manny seemed surprised.

"Are you sure?"

"No, but close it before I change my mind," Fernando said.

Just then Antonio walked into his office. "I thought you quit smoking?"

"I did." He offered the pack to Antonio, who took a cigarette and lit it and then inhaled deeply.

While they smoked he told Antonio about his meeting with Rose and her version of the events leading up to Kim's murder.

"Do you believe her?"

Fernando shrugged. "There were some discrepancies. Rose said Kim and Jimmy were both screaming, while June Bryan sleeping next door said she heard nothing when Kim arrived. Also Rose said Kim was the one who went up to the studio to get the knife, but it's probably more likely that Rose grabbed it to protect herself from Kim and Jimmy, both of whom were raging drunk that night. We know for a fact that Jimmy was a mean drunk. I don't know about Kim."

"So then you believe her, more or less?" Antonio asked.

"Yeah, but who knows? Hers is the only version we have. The other two people involved are both dead."

"Unless the Mayor was there," Antonio said.

"I doubt that. No one mentioned him being present that night, including June. Plus, say what you will about Martin, he seems too smart to be involved in a murder scene."

"Smart enough to hire someone else to do his killing, you mean," Antonio added.

"Exactly."

Fernando put his emergency pack of Camel Lights back in the drawer and closed it tight. Maybe he'd have one more when this day concluded.

"Okay," Fernando said. "Let's pay the Mayor a visit and find out what he has to say about the two gunmen. I want to hear his explanation. This will be my last play."

Antonio followed him down the hallway and outside. They walked down to Lincoln and over to city hall. Inside they found several people sitting in the hallway waiting to talk to the Mayor. The Mayor's personal bodyguard stood outside the office door. Al didn't look happy to see them, avoiding eye contact as they walked up to the door. Then when he saw what they were about to do, he raised his arm to stop them from entering.

Fernando pushed Al's arm away.

Antonio followed, looking down and scowling at the confused bodyguard. "You! Stay out in the hallway."

"Keep him out of the office, Antonio," Fernando said.

"My pleasure." Antonio pointed to a chair in the waiting room. "Sit down and shut up."

Al did as he was told, intimidated by the big man who was a good ten inches taller and seventy pounds heavier.

Fernando threw open the door and burst into the Mayor's office. Martin, surprised, jumped up in his seat, mouth open as though he were about to say something. He didn't.

Fernando walked to the center of the room and stood there glaring at the Mayor. "Surprised to see me?"

"Lopez...I was just about to call you...thank you for the work you've done on my wife's case."

"Yeah? Then why did you send your two goons after us?" Fernando asked.

"That was a mistake," Martin said, looking nervously at the office door as if expecting Al to come to his assistance. "They were supposed to discourage you, not harm you. They went too far. They overplayed their hand."

"Yeah, and they paid the price. Now it's your turn. I thought you were a better politician than to pull something as crude as this."

"I swear this was all a mistake, a misunderstanding," Martin said.

"What about Jimmy?"

"Same. They were only supposed to find Jimmy and lead you to him, so he would be arrested for Kim's murder."

"In order to protect Rose...who you were fucking," Fernando said.

Martin's face turned bright red. "Yes, because Kim's death was an accident. Nobody was really responsible. Kim was sloppy drunk. She and Rose quarreled and then Kim went to get a knife. The two of them wrestled, and somehow the knife ended up in Kim's chest. Rose panicked. She tried to get Jimmy to call Nine One One but he refused. He was sloppy drunk, like Kim. He did nothing. He let Kim bleed out sitting in her car waiting for someone to help her. So who's to blame? Kim for starting the argument? Rose for fighting back? Jimmy for not calling an ambulance when he might have saved Kim's life? You see what I mean? No one's to blame."

Fernando frowned. "Or everyone's to blame."

"Accidents and misunderstandings, an unfortunate chain of events," Martin said, starting to plead now. "I don't know how else to describe it. None of this was intentional. Rose didn't intend to harm Kim, and I certainly didn't intend to harm Jimmy or the two of you when I hired security. Don't you see?"

Fernando said nothing. He continued to stare at Martin.

"Look...I fucked up," Martin said, suddenly deflated, realizing Al would not be coming to his rescue. "But even if you took the case to Steve Chabot he wouldn't bring charges against Rose. He has no case, no evidence, only her version of events. Jimmy bears as much responsibility as Rose for Kim's death since he refused to call Nine One One. More responsibility really, because unlike Rose his action was intentional. And Jimmy's dead. End of case. We can all move on with our lives. Don't you see?"

"Except for Kim and Jimmy and the two dead security guards," Fernando said.

"Listen...if you arrest Rose, the only thing you'll accomplish will be to damage her reputation and probably her future. Why do that?"

"And what about you?"

"Same thing," Martin said. "The two guys who killed Jimmy are both dead. End of case."

"Not quite. There was a third person involved. You!"

Martin squirmed in his seat. "Please. I'm asking you to let it go.

Walk away and let Manny close the case. Nothing would be gained by pursuing this. You would only damage more people's reputations."

"You mean your reputation," Fernando said.

"Mine, yes, but others too. And even if you took the case to the District Attorney, he wouldn't file charges. You don't have the evidence."

"Not true. We have all the evidence we need."

"What do you mean?" Martin asked.

"From Tom Spain and Duane Jackson, the two security guards you sent to kill us," Fernando said. "Do you even remember their names? We have their cell phones and a record of all the calls they made to your office. We have an envelope containing ten thousand dollars in cash and a handwritten note, and we have copies of emails sent to them from your office. More than enough to send you away for a very long time."

Now Martin began to panic. His face turned red. "I'm asking you, Fernando. Please don't put everyone through this. It was all an accident, a series of accidents and misunderstandings. Please believe me. None of this was intentional. A big fuck-up. Rose, me, the two idiots who killed Jimmy. We all made mistakes...."

Fernando raised his hand. "Enough! Here's what's going to happen. You're going to call your press secretary and tell her you intend to hold a press conference tomorrow morning and announce your resignation as Mayor effective immediately because of personal reasons--your wife's death. If you don't do this, I'll take all the evidence to the Federal Prosecutor in Albuquerque. Scott Anderson will know what to do with it. He has zero tolerance for corrupt politicians. Do you understand?"

Martin nodded.

"You'll not only lose your reputation, you'll spend a considerable amount of time in federal prison. I hear corrupt politicians are not real popular in federal prisons."

"Okay...I'll resign."

He pointed to the telephone on Martin's desk. "Call your press secretary now."

Martin picked up the phone and called Beth Williams, his press secretary, and told her to set up a press conference tomorrow morning so he could announce his resignation.

Martin put down the phone and looked at him. "I'm sorry, Fernando."

Fernando frowned. "Everyone's sorry. Everyone's looking for absolution."

Martin sighed but said nothing.

"Well, you'll have to find it elsewhere," Fernando said.

With that Fernando turned and walked out of the office, leaving the Mayor slouched in his chair. His work was finished. Finally.

38

Ruby called less than fifteen minutes after the Mayor announced his resignation at a hastily called news conference next morning. He was sitting on the back patio reading the morning *Independent* and drinking his third cup of coffee, a free man since he'd signed on the dotted line and basically told the Chief, the District Attorney, and everyone else in the department to fuck off.

"Fernando, you sly fox," Ruby said. "How did you do it? I want to know all the details."

He laughed. "It's a long story. Too long to tell over the phone."

"Then meet me at Emilio's for lunch, say eleven-thirty. My treat."

"I'll be there."

He finished reading the newspaper and then went for a long walk along Acequia Madre, trying to decide if he liked the idea of being retired. What the hell would he do if he didn't work? Antonio was always inviting him up to his cabin to hike and fish in the Pecos, but the thought of hiking in a national forest exhausted him. And as for fishing, he'd given up that years ago, when his fishing line had gotten tangled in a bunch of weeds at Cochiti Lake and he'd thrown the damn rod and reel into the lake. Unlike Estelle, gardening bored him after about an hour. Reading bored him, except for the *Independent*. That just pissed him off. Everything bored him except working, which kept him from thinking about being bored.

The idea occurred to him that maybe he could put up his shingle as a private eye. Rent an office somewhere in town, maybe on Cerrillos Road or one of the seedier parts of Santa Fe. If he became a private dick, he could take only the cases that interested him. The more he thought about it, the more he liked the idea. Estelle would be the only problem. She would object and accuse him of going back on his long-standing promise to retire. But a private dick was different, he told himself. He could stay away from the dangerous cases. Estelle might approve of that.

He spent the rest of the morning thinking about the logistics of his plan and then drove down to the Railyard to meet Ruby for lunch. He parked in front of her pottery co-op and walked inside Emilio's, where he saw her sitting in the back booth talking to Emilio. Emilio wore what looked like the same dirty apron he wore the last time Fernando was here. The apron pooched out over his huge belly.

"I ordered my usual salad. What'll you have?" Ruby asked as he took a seat in the booth across from her.

"Same with me, I'll stick with my usual. Just give me a bowl of posole and a couple of warm tortillas, please," Fernando said.

Emilio took their orders and disappeared.

Ruby stared at him. "So, Fernando, how did you do it? How did you force the Mayor to resign?"

"Force? Not exactly. I just convinced him it was in his best interest to step down."

"Yeah? How?" Ruby asked.

Fernando told her about the two gunmen who killed Jimmy and who attempted to kill him and Antonio. "Turns out they were hired by Martin. We found what evidence we needed in their van: their cell phones, a copy of an email from the Mayor's office, and an envelope filled with cash accompanied by a handwritten note from the Mayor's bodyguard."

She stifled a laugh. "The Mayor hired two assassins?"

"Well, they listed themselves as security guards," Fernando said. "Martin claims they were only supposed to intimidate us but went rogue."

She looked surprised. "And you managed to get access to their computers and cell phones this quickly?"

"No...but I made him think I'd accessed the devices, which made him nervous. That's how I knew the computers and cell phones contained compromising information. So I offered him a deal: if he resigned, I wouldn't take the information to the Federal Prosecutor in Albuquerque. If he refused to resign, I would deliver the goods to the Feds."

"And he believed you?" Ruby asked.

"He didn't want to take a chance," Fernando said. "Do you blame him?"

She laughed. "Like I said, you are one sly fox."

"Sometimes you win, sometimes you lose."

"You know...?" Ruby started and then stopped.

"What?" Fernando asked.

"Maybe I'll run for Mayor again. I only lost by a few hundred votes last time. Maybe the city is ready for another woman Mayor. Lord knows, the men have been such miserable pricks."

"Okay, but you'll have to clean up your language," Fernando said, laughing.

She looked at him askance. "What, are you my campaign manager now?"

"Remember what happened on the Council."

"Bunch of clowns, the whole lot of them," Ruby said. "And you know what? They get worse every year."

"Posole and a house salad," Emilio announced, and set their lunches on the table. "Can I get you anything to drink? Coffee? Tea? Beer?"

Neither of them ordered anything to drink.

"So, Ruby, tell me the truth. What did Rose tell you about the night Kim died? Did she tell you about her fight with Kim...with the knife?"

She frowned. "She told me the basics. To be honest, I didn't really want to know the details. Too depressing"

"Then why didn't you tell me earlier?"

"I thought she should be the one to tell you," Ruby said. "It was her decision, not mine. She fucked up, so it was on her to come clean."

"But who started the fight?" Fernando asked. "Who went up to the studio to get the knife?"

Ruby shrugged. "I don't know. Probably Kim, since she was more volatile. But that's just a guess. They were both jealous of each other."

"Jealous?"

"Of course. Kim was jealous of Rose because Rose was pleasing her husband in bed, something she couldn't do. And Rose was jealous of Kim because Kim was sleeping with everyone else."

"Just life on Canyon Road, eh?" Fernando asked.

"You got that right."

After a long silence, Fernando asked, "So what are you going to do with Jimmy's studio? He left everything to you in his will."

"I don't know. Maybe sell it. Maybe make it my own gallery. Why do you ask?"

"Now that I'm retired from the department I'm thinking about going into business for myself," Fernando said. "As a private investigator. If I do, I'll need an office. Where better to have an office than Canyon Road."

"Hah! Lotta divorce work anyway."

"Exactly."

Ruby nodded. "Sure, you're welcome to use the garage. It has its own door and side windows for light. You could even bring in a contractor and have them fix it up however you want, like a real office. Hang your shingle outside and you'd be ready for business."

"I might take you up on that, if the rent's not too steep."

"No rent. Just pay your share of the utilities and we'll call it even."

"Thanks, Ruby. Very generous of you."

"Matter of fact I could use the security," she said. "I have a lot of enemies, you know."

He laughed. "I do know."

Ruby smiled. "Almost as many as you."

Readers Guide

1. Santa Fe artist Jimmy Mackey drinks a bit. What else explains his quirky, eccentric personality?

2. Jimmy wakes up with a massive hangover after a night of heavy drinking at his studio with his Canyon Road friends. His morning gets worse when a police car pulls into his parking lot and even worse when they find a dead woman in the trunk of an abandoned car next to his studio. The woman turns out to be the Santa Fe mayor's estranged wife, Kim Martin. Why do the Santa Fe Police suspect Jimmy is the murderer?

3. As the story begins Detective Fernando Lopez is on medical leave pending retirement as a result of injuries received during his last homicide case in Chaco Canyon (see *Ghost Canyon*). Chief of Police Larry Stuart calls on Fernando and asks him to take the Kim Martin case. Why do Fernando and Chief Stuart have a strained relationship? Given that, why does Stuart turn to Fernando?

4. Describe the collection of artists and gallery owners that inhabit Jimmy's world on Canyon Road: Ruby Montez, Blaine Rogers, Rose Lucero, and Paul and June Bryan. Who among them might be reliable as narrators or sources of information?

5. Describe Jimmy's relationship with his latest ex-wife, Ruby Montez. Why do so many women love Jimmy at the same time they hate him? What's Jimmy's secret?

6. Detective Lopez and his colleague Antonio Blake finally catch up with Jimmy at Ghost Ranch, near Abiquiu, N.M. Where does Ghost Ranch get its name? Why is Detective Lopez reluctant to go there?

7. At Ghost Ranch Jimmy is accompanied by Blaine Rogers, who sells Jimmy's paintings in his art gallery. Why has Rogers come to Ghost Ranch? Does he have an ulterior motive?

8. After Jimmy escapes at Ghost Ranch, he turns up in the town of Taos, New Mexico, where he is assassinated by two gunmen at the home of another of his ex-wives. Afterwards Chief Stuart and Santa Fe Mayor Joe Martin tell Detective Lopez to drop the Kim Martin investigation immediately. Why does that raise a red flag for Detective Lopez?

9. Detective Lopez conducts multiple interviews with the people who were drinking at Jimmy's studio the night Kim Martin was murdered. Which of Jimmy's friends provide the key bits of evidence that allow Detective Lopez to solve the mystery of who killed Kim Martin? Explain.

10. What does Raoul Garcia, a high-powered Santa Fe lawyer famous for successfully defending guilty clients, tell Detective Lopez he should do? Does he comply?

11. What decisions about crime and punishment does Detective Lopez make at the end of the mystery? Why? Has his sense of justice changed in the course of the investigation?

www.ingramcontent.com/pod-product-compliance
Lightning Source LLC
Chambersburg PA
CBHW010357310726
48979CB00006B/1077

* 9 7 8 1 6 3 2 9 3 4 4 9 9 *